Surrendering to the Baron

By Georgette Brown

COPYRIGHT

Surrendering to the Baron

Chapter One

LEOPOLD SPENCER, THE FIFTH Baron Ramsay, felt the blow in his groin, as if one of the steeds currently rounding the straightaway had kicked him in the bollocks. He lowered his field glasses and tried to address his friend with calm. "Where is it you say our wives are staying?"

"Château Follet," Charles responded a little louder over the noise of the grandstands. "Or some demmed Frenchie name. By Jove, the Turk took that turn well! I think my judgment of horseflesh can finally rival yours, eh?"

Though the Royal Ascot meeting was the purpose of the day for Leopold, with the Gold Cup yet to follow on Ladies' Day, a more important matter now held his attention captive. Charles knew not that Château Follet was also known by the name of Château Debauchery, or he would not have spoken of the place with such indifference.

"Your wife, Diana, told you this?" Leopold asked.

"Yes, she was rambling away, as wives will do, about which shops and millineries they would patronize whilst in London. Dreadful dull matters that can only interest the fair sex. I told her that, with enough changing of the horses, she could make the trip to town in one day, but she thought the journey might prove too taxing for *your* wife. Said that this Château Follet was the perfect place to spend the night—possibly two, as she is well acquainted with the lady of the house."

The impish little vixen. Leopold felt his groin tighten. It surprised him little if Diana, his cousin, knowing full well her husband never listened to her with more than half an ear, should deliberately flaunt the name of Château Follet, a den of debauchery where men and women engaged in pleasures of the flesh. He had not thought Diana would return there after marrying Charles. Though Leopold had always enjoyed his visits to Follet, he had forsaken the place after marrying Trudie two years ago.

Good God. Trudie. Was she aware of what transpired at the Château? It was too incredible that his shy and awkward wife should know of, let alone venture into, such a place. The wicked wantonness there would surely horrify her.

Of a sudden, he recalled an unremarkable conversation between them at the breakfast table a fortnight ago, when Trudie had announced that she and Diana wished to travel to London to purchase fabrics for the latest fashion plates.

"As—as you and Charles will be at the races," Trudie had said, the pitch of her voice higher than usual, "we ladies will have a bit of our own fun in town."

He had nodded and politely inquired where they were staying and the length of their stay, though, in truth, he had been more interested in returning to his newspaper at the time.

"I—we—Diana has arranged the, er, particulars."

She had not met his eye and was instead fixed upon applying a fifth coat of jam to her toast. Trudie had none of the guiles that many others of her sex perfected. Her eyes of cornflower blue, often wide with naiveté, could hold no falsehood. She was artless, a quality the late Mrs. Spencer had often extolled in recommending Trudie Bonneville to her son. The eldest of three, Trudie was also responsible and sensible. Leopold respected all these traits.

And found them rather dull.

But perhaps Trudie was not as sensible as he would have thought. They had been married two years, though, as his mother and hers were the best of friends, he had known Trudie since she was in leading strings.

When he had gone off to Eton and then Oxford, he had seen little of her during her maturation into a young woman. Nonetheless, as she still possessed the rounded cheeks of her childhood and appeared no more comfortable in the attire of a woman than she did in the lace-frilled gowns her mother used to always adorn her with, he saw the same girl who would hide behind the sofa with a plateful of biscuits, unaware that the powdered sugar masking half her face betrayed what she had been about.

He never would have selected Trudie for himself— she was middling in appearance and wit—but it was his mother's dearest wish before her death to have the two families united.

"I think your luck has taken a turn for the worse, Leo," Charles said with a nudge. "Your horse has fallen half a lap behind."

Leopold looked out over the tracks. His steed did appear to struggle, but losing a hundred guineas was hardly important now. He cursed himself, for, as he reviewed the days prior to his departure for Ascot, to be followed by his wife's departure for London the following day, he now saw that Trudie had been ill at ease all those days. She had hardly looked him in the eye. Though she was prone to fidgeting, as if the pins in her gown poked her constantly, she could hardly sit still at the dining table. She ate quickly and often asked to be excused.

The greatest evidence of her nerves, however, lay in her favorite pastime, the pianoforte. Trudie excelled at the instrument and could play for hours. He knew her to be attempting a new concerto—the one in C Major by Mozart, he believed—but she had been unable to play through pieces that she had mastered years ago.

Her odd behavior had not attracted his notice at the time, but now he viewed it with great foreboding, for why would she display such disquiet lest she well knew what Château Follet was about?

He had not thought to hear its name again, though Diana had once teased him, suggesting that the *four* of them could have a ribald time there, but he had quickly quelled such a notion. Trudie was far from comfortable in the bedchamber. Their wedding night had been quite the disaster for both of them. He had been as gentle as he could, and she had tried to contain her cries, but it was evident to him that she took no pleasure in their congress. He had hoped, after the initial pain, that subsequent attempts would prove more agreeable to her, but she had looked ready to leap from the bed at his every touch.

She would never engage in any of the activities at the Château Follet. Surely Diana, one of her dearest friends, knew this? The two women talked often, and their sex had a habit of leaving no subject unturned.

But then why were they headed to Follet? What could Diana intend but to make cuckolds of him and Charles? He knew Diana to be discontented in her marriage, but would Trudie acquiesce to adultery? He would not have thought it possible, but as he reflected on the past sennight, she had been behaving with all the indications of a guilty conscience.

Granted, he himself had not been faithful in the last year, though he did not brandish his affairs as Charles did. He was not a poor husband, in that he never spoke a harsh word to Trudie and always treated her with courtesy and kindness. She knew as well as he that their marriage served to satisfy their families. Their mothers had crafted their engagement at their births. The Bonnevilles had wealth, and the Spencers had breeding. Both families benefited from the match.

The excitement of the crowd rose, with Charles cheering loudly, as the horses came into the final lap. Leopold glanced at Charles, wondering if he should inform his friend of the need to depart Berkshire immediately to rescue their wives. Charles would be livid and want to lock Diana in her chambers, perhaps more cross at being pulled away from the races than at his wife's infidelity.

Leopold decided he could fetch the two women and bring them home himself. The responsibility to inform Charles would then rest appropriately with Diana.

It was a good day's journey to Château Follet, but if he departed within the hour, he could arrive before the women had to spend the night.

Charles leaped in triumph as the horses crossed the finish line. "Damn me, the Turk won! He won!"

After celebrating with the fellow beside him, who had made the same fortunate bet, Charles turned back to Leopold. "Here now, I know your horse finished down the field, but you look as if you lost more than a hundred quid. The day is young. You may recoup your losses yet. Lest your wife overspends her allowance, eh? I know Diana will with hers."

Leopold managed a grim smile. "I shall have to take my losses for the day. I fear I have neglected a matter that, upon reflection, requires some urgency to resolve."

Charles stared at him. "Eh?"

"Make my bets for me while I am gone and keep the winnings if there are any to be had."

Knowing this to be an offer Charles could not refuse, Leopold took his leave. He ought to trust that Trudie, once she realized what Château Follet was about, would turn upon her heel in an instant to seek safer shelter. Surely Marguerite Follet, the proprietress, would see that Trudie was not a suitable guest.

But he could not risk it. And, perhaps, locking one's wife in her chambers might yet prove an appealing option.

Chapter Two

LEOPOLD PACED THE ANTEROOM of Marguerite Follet's boudoir. Little had changed since last he had stayed at the Château Follet some years ago. Despite a palpable nostalgia for the place, he was far from happy over the circumstances that currently compelled his presence. The roads to Château Follet had been favorable, and he had made good time, but throughout the journey he had felt the impending cuckoldry in the depths of his loins. Diana may not have provided specifics to her description of the château, but she could not have expected to conceal its purpose from Trudie. Given his wife's recent behavior, it was more than likely she had agreed to the affair. Leopold had inventoried all the men Trudie knew. None appeared the obvious offender. If she had been unfaithful, she had hid it well, though he had never known her to be deceitful till now. He knew the hypocrisy of condemning Trudie for her faithlessness when he himself entertained a mistress, but her choice of the Château Follet for her tryst riled for reasons he could not name.

"She should not be here," he insisted to Madame Follet after being admitted to her room.

The proprietress stood in her negligee while a chambermaid assisted with her toilette. Though his senior by many years, Madame Follet wore her age with grace and elegance, aided by eyes that sparkled with vigor, a smooth and pale complexion, and a trim figure. She narrowed her eyes at his hasty speech.

Recalling his manners, he quickly bowed and kissed her hand. "Your pardon, Madame. *Comment allez-vous?*"

"Leopold Spencer," she remembered, her gaze sweeping over him with obvious appreciation of what she saw. "*Je vais bien.* Now, of whom do you speak?"

"My wife."

She raised a brow. "You are not arrived together?"

"She came without my knowledge."

"Lost the reins to your wife, have we, Lord Ramsay?"

He bristled.

"Rather a surprise," she continued as she examined the different pairs of stockings offered by the maid. "I remember you as quite the *dominant.*"

He had fond memories of Château Follet but, for some reason, had not thought to bring his mistress here.

Marguerite lowered her lashes. "As you know, we've plenty of leashes here."

"My marriage is not that sort of arrangement," he said, though the thought of clapping a leash on Trudie was not wholly objectionable, especially if she were inclined to run off on wild and irresponsible ventures.

"How unfortunate. I know not your wife, but she must be the flaxen-haired young lady who arrived with your cousin?"

"Were they accompanied by anyone or did they rendezvous with another guest?"

"I am not aware of their plans, *mon chéri.*"

"I want them sent home."

"Lord Ramsay, you may take up the mantle of master with your wife as it pleases you, but do not require my intervention."

"They know not what they are about. This is no place for Trudie," he maintained, and began to pace once more.

She looked at him sharply. "I invite all manner of women to enjoy themselves here."

"I meant no offense, Madame, but I think my wife to be entirely naïve as to what transpires here. Château Follet is beyond her."

Marguerite sat down at her vanity and began applying her powder. "A bold insistence by someone caught unawares of his wife's whereabouts."

"Trudie is the last person I would expect to find here."

"It would seem that you do not completely know your wife."

A muscle tightened along his jaw.

She looked at him through the mirror. "If you mean to rescue your wife from the treachery of Château Follet—"

"Madame, you must know I have only fond recollections of my time here, but Trudie is…inexperienced."

"If you wish to claim her, I shall not prevent you. But the hour is late and you have but arrived. My groomsman Jacque is at your disposal, and there are many guest chambers available. I invite you to make yourself comfortable. You are welcome to stay the night—or two. I do believe Diana and your wife are staying at least two."

At least *two?* he nearly bellowed. Instead, he said with comportment, "I am honored by your invitation but, regretfully, I cannot accept."

"Are you so certain the women will go with you?"

"I cannot force Diana to leave with me, but I will take my wife."

"And install her under lock and key so that she never returns?"

Leopold squared his shoulders. He had not yet pondered that possibility. A proper scolding should dissuade Trudie from ever considering a second visit to Follet…but what if it did not?

"Madame, will you not explain to my wife—"

"*Certainement no.* You would ask me to criticize my own residence?"

"I beg your pardon! That is not what I intended. I only meant that you could, with your vast experience, dissuade Trudie and convince her that she would find Château Follet most unsuitable."

"But I know not your wife. And I will say to you what I said to an overbearing marquess last week: that I find it rather selfish of you to deny her the pleasures that you have partaken readily of here at Château

13

Follet."

Her words jolted him, especially when he had considered himself quite magnanimous for not condemning his wife her infidelity. His intention in coming to the Château was to *protect* Trudie.

Marguerite softened her tone. "Given your absence from the Château, perhaps you should consider making up for lost time. It would please me much if you chose to stay."

She held out her hand, a clear signal of dismissal. He pressed his lips to her hand. There was little to be done but accept her offer for the moment.

Ensconced in one of the guest chambers, he dismissed Jacque soon after the groomsman had assisted him out of his coat and boots. He went to the sideboard and poured a glass of brandy. He finished the beverage rather quickly, then poured himself another. He gazed at the painting on the opposite wall. Scantily clad nymphs, many with their nipples showing through their thin garments, danced with satyrs in a forest setting.

He settled into an armchair facing the four-post bed. His last time here, he had a lovely maiden tied between those posts, moaning and writhing with delight to his bedchamber skills. His surroundings and the brandy sank in, warming his blood. A shame he would not be able to partake in the events of the Château. But his mission was clear.

It was unfortunate that Marguerite was not willing to accommodate his request. Who better than the proprietress herself to convince Trudie of the inappropriateness of the Château? And she would have spared Trudie the embarrassment of facing her husband, though he took some gratification at the thought of witnessing his wife's mortification. Surely she would think twice about deceiving him and running off to places such as the Château Follet!

Now he had no option but to remove Trudie from the château himself. If he marched himself into her chambers, she would be too surprised and shamefaced to protest. But, as he had voiced to Marguerite, there was no guarantee that Trudie would not simply return at a later time.

He glanced at the longcase clock opposite him. The hour was indeed late. He had no affinity for traveling at night, and it would be too dangerous for a woman. He could claim his wife now, before any of the evening's activities took place, but he admitted a growing curiosity to know the extent of her infidelity and whether she would truly consent to the debauchery here. He could not imagine Trudie would tolerate the wanton exhibition and forays into debauchery when she could ill handle the overtures of her own husband, but it had been over a year since he had approached her. Perhaps it was best to keep a furtive profile and depart on the morrow. He could keep an eye on Trudie to ensure her safety *and* discern who her possible paramour might be.

He rose and went to the armoire. Opening its doors, he found a selection of face masks. He picked a simple half mask of black satin. A matching black banyan hung beside it. The lighting at the Château was always dim, but he chose a powdered wig to further disguise himself from recognition.

As he donned the articles, he felt a strange anticipation.

Chapter Three

HIS WIFE WAS NOWHERE to be found.

"Are you quite certain she is not in her chambers?" Leopold inquired of the maidservant he had asked to search the rooms.

"Yes, m'lord," the woman replied.

"But her effects are still there? She has not departed?"

"Her portmanteau remains unpacked."

Leopold returned downstairs to the assembly room, where the pairing ritual was held for guests to claim their partners. He saw Diana upon the lap of a handsome rogue, and thought of Charles joyfully watching the races, oblivious to his wife's infidelity. Engrossed in murmuring into her paramour's ear, she took no notice of Leopold. Even if she had, she would likely not have recognized him behind his mask and wig. He was tempted to ask Diana, who ought to have, as she had brought Trudie here, looked after her friend.

"Was she here?" Leopold asked of Madame Follet, who sat with her legs stretched upon a sofa while a young man several years her junior held a glass of wine to her lips.

"I've not seen the baroness since supper," she

replied after a sip. "I do hope she is well and can partake a little of the pleasures of the night. I would have tended to her more, but since you are here, I thought it unnecessary."

"Are all your guests accounted for here?"

She looked about the room. "I think a few have left to begin the true start of their evenings."

Leopold knew not how to receive the information. When first he had entered the assembly room earlier to see with whom Trudie might engage in criminal congress, he had been relieved to find her absent. Perhaps she had come to her senses and had chosen instead to retire for the evening. That she was not in her chambers left open the possibility that she might have gone off with one of the guests. It concerned him. She could not possibly fathom what transpired here at Château Follet, even if Diana had provided the most detailed of descriptions. Hearing of the activities was not the same as experiencing them.

And what of the man who would claim her? Would he be kind and gentle? Would he perceive her awkwardness and how easily she could be discomfited?

Leaving the assembly room, Leopold renewed his urgency to find Trudie. As he went through empty room after empty room on the first floor of the château, he began to consider how he might search the bedchambers upstairs without bursting in upon unsuspecting guests, but there was no way to prevent such an event if he was to be thorough in his search. And he would not rest until he had found Trudie.

After he discovered her safe and unharmed, he would be tempted to give her the proper scolding she deserved. It mattered not if she had come to Château Follet at Diana's urging. In coming, Trudie had acquiesced to committing adultery. She had acquiesced to making him a cuckold.

His anger should be tempered, he knew, by guilt over his own infidelity, but wives could not be made cuckolds. He had done his duty in marrying Trudie, had treated her with nothing but kindness, had seen that she had more than enough in the way of pin money and had never denied her anything of consequence. That he did not often visit her bed was likely a relief for her. And she would repay all this by making him a cuckold.

As he allowed his anger to stew, he heard music coming from behind the partially closed doors of a drawing room. Looking through the opening, he beheld a woman seated at a pianoforte, her back to him. Like him, she wore the fashion of the prior century. Her satin dress of dark indigo had petticoats that made her full hips appear even more ample. Her hair was done in a powdered coiffure, but he recognized her figure.

Entering, he stood at the threshold and listened. A skilled *pianiste*, Trudie often liked to challenge herself with difficult pieces. At present, she played the "Sonata in E-flat Major" by Joseph Haydn. The large composition reflected much of the composer's late complexities and sophistication. At the instrument, she commanded a passion that did not appear in her demeanor. Or perhaps he had simply not noticed it before.

She finished the final notes with flourish. Having been engrossed in the music, she nearly fell off the bench at the sound of him clapping. She scrambled to her feet and nearly knocked the bench over. She steadied the seat before standing behind the far end of the bench. Though she wore a Venetian mask over her eyes, he knew by her movements that it was Trudie.

"You're an accomplished player," he remarked in low, hushed tones to disguise his voice.

"Th-Thank you," she replied. She pulled at the sleeve of her gown, where layers of lace descended from the elbow. Knowing his wife, she could not be comfortable in such a garment. She adjusted the mask as she cleared her throat.

"Do you await someone here?" he asked.

"No, I—I passed by the room quite by accident and saw this instrument, a Broadwood, and I could not resist."

He eyed the beautifully grained rosewood and mahogany beside her. In addition to its stately harpsichord case, the instrument produced more resonance than the Viennese she had at home.

"The other guests are gathered in the assembly room," he said.

"Yes, I know."

"If you are alone at the château, you may acquire a partner there."

She drew in a sharp breath and nodded.

"But you must hurry," he added. "Some of the

guests have dispersed already."

"Thank you, but I think—I think I shall retire for the evening."

He was relieved but raised his brows. Could she possibly have come for no reason other than to keep Diana company? "Retire? The night is young yet."

"Yes, well, I had a rather long day of travel."

She scratched at her hair, and he imagined the powder to itch considerably. It would have been no easy task to outfit herself in the fashion of Marie Antoinette. Why undertake all that effort for naught?

"Nevertheless," he replied, "one does not venture to Château Follet to *rest*."

His comment must have made her uneasy. She seemed not to know where to look.

"I did not think I would feel as fatigued as I do," she answered at last. He could tell she was perturbed by his prodding but was too polite to call out his impertinence.

"Then you did have, at least, the intention to avail yourself of the offerings here."

"Your pardon?"

"This must be your first visit to Château Follet."

"Yes. It is a lovely estate."

"May I ask how you came to know of it?"

"My friend. She is acquainted with Madame Follet."

"And she told you what transpires here?"

Trudie stared at him with brows knitted. Undoubtedly, she was trying to place the motive for his questioning. "Yes."

"Are you acquainted with anyone else here?"

"If—if you will not find me rude, sir, I do think I should retire."

She waited for him to respond, but as he did not move, she remained where she was.

"Your friend left you to fend for yourself?" he tried.

"Did Madame Follet send you, sir, to inquire after me?" Trudie replied.

"She was concerned that you would not enjoy yourself properly."

She let out the breath she held. "Please tell Madame that I much appreciate her hospitality but regret that I cannot avail myself of the, er, festivities offered."

"Why not?"

"I find myself fatigued."

He caught the irk she tried to keep out of her tone. "Is that all?"

"Sir, I am in earnest and will bid you good night."

If he were to act the gentleman, he would bow and step aside. She was waiting for just such a motion, but he remained where he was. Upon stepping into Château Follet, one divested the mantle of gentleman and lady.

Flustered, Trudie looked about as if seeking another means of escape. Unaccustomed to wearing such voluminous petticoats, she tugged at her skirts. She stopped. "Will you not miss the pairing event yourself, sir?"

Leopold grinned to himself at her attempt to rid herself of him. "I have no interest in the pairing."

"Oh," she responded with disappointment. "Why, then, are you at Château Follet?"

"I came to retrieve something of mine."

"Ah, well, I pray you will convey my apologies to Madame Follet, and, as the hour is late for me——"

"You're married," he said, directing his gaze at her wedding ring. He had taken care to remove his when changing.

She thrust her right hand over the left. "I understand it to be of little consequence here at the château."

"None," he affirmed. "Nonetheless, you must be discontented in your marriage to come here, lest you came with your husband."

Her bottom lip quivered. He had clearly touched a nerve.

She squared her shoulders. "What marriage is not touched by discontent?"

Her response, though arch, lacked conviction. He took a step farther into the room. "So your husband is not here. Have you a paramour here?"

She retreated a step. He could see her mind churning to find the appropriate response. He had never known Trudie to prevaricate—till recently—and a less mannered woman would have called him out for his prying.

"No," she answered. "Did Madame Follet request these questions?"

It was a poor attempt to put him in his place. Finding her response rather droll, he took another step forward. "I merely think it curious that one would come all this way to Château Follet and *not* partake of its purpose. Do the activities frighten you?"

She retreated a step. "A little. They are...beyond what I am accustomed to."

"But they interest you."

"My friend persuaded me that it would be a fine experience."

He pressed his lips into a line. It would seem she had, at one point, considered her participation at Follet. "Do you believe her?"

Trudie faltered. "Sir, you ask questions of a rather intimate nature."

"You were ready to submit yourself—your body—to a perfect stranger. My questions are harmless in comparison."

He should have been relieved that she had opted to go to bed instead of pursuing a liaison, but he found himself wanting to know how far she would have gone if she were not fatigued as claimed. He advanced another step.

"Do you believe your friend?" he tried again.

"I believe—I believe her knowledgeable in these matters," she said. "She has been here before and praised the enjoyment of it."

"And you wished to sample the pleasures here for yourself." At her guilty expression, he felt both a wave of sympathy and anger at her willing betrayal. "Worry not. As one who has indulged in the offerings here many a time, it would be hypocritical of me to censure you. Indeed, I praise your pursuit of the fleshly pleasures. Much courage is required, particularly of your sex."

Her countenance softened. "It—it would have been an adventure unlike any for me."

"The adventure can still be had."

She fussed with the lace at her décolletage. He eyed the lush swell of her breasts and felt a tug at his groin.

"Perhaps, after a cup of tea or coffee, you can overcome your fatigue," he said. "Why come all this way to return empty-handed?"

She did not refute his reasoning and lowered her gaze in thought, but then she shook her head. "I could not."

"Why not?"

"I know no one here."

"There can be much titillation in lying with a stranger."

"Yes, Dian—my friend, said the same."

"And you are inclined to believe her, are you not?"

"But I am married."

A muscle rippled along his jaw. That had not stopped her from coming to Château Follet, but he kept his tone friendly. "Your husband does not note your absence?"

"He enjoys the races at Ascot. He would not miss me."

The latter sentence was murmured as if to herself, but he heard the resignation in her voice. "Indeed?"

She seemed surprised that he had heard. "Yes, well, he—he has a mistress to satisfy him."

It was his turn to be surprised. He had not known

that Trudie knew. He had taken care that she would not.

"Are you certain of this?" he asked, searching her countenance for emotion. Was she saddened or vexed by his mistress? To his surprise, he found neither sorrow nor anger but a calm acceptance of his infidelity.

She nodded. "My friend—her husband made mention of it to her quite by accident."

Charles. Leopold suppressed an oath. He should have known Charles had as large a mouth as Diana.

"Hearsay does not qualify as verity."

"Well, I—I saw her—his mistress, that is."

"How unfortunate," Leopold said carefully, "that your husband should flaunt his mistress before his own wife."

"Oh, he did not! I arrived at London last season a day earlier than I had told him I would. When I was told he had gone to the theater, I followed suit and saw him—them. She is quite pretty. Beautiful, rather."

Stunned, Leopold stared at her. His wife had lied to him more than once? What else had she hid from him? Seeing the sadness now in her eyes, he put aside the queries for now. He cursed himself. He had hoped to spare Trudie the pain of knowing—had even convinced himself at one point that she would hardly care that he had a mistress because she had demonstrated so little interest in the amorous attentions of her husband. Many a husband entertained mistresses, and their wives either did not know or chose to look the other way.

But a part of him had always known such attempts to convince himself of the harmlessness of what he did to be false. He had feared that Trudie would be hurt. If she had been more receptive of him in bed, he might not have felt as compelled to take a mistress. But it mattered not how much fault could be placed at her door. He could not rid himself of the remorse.

"I can see why a man, wed or not, would wish to keep her company," Trudie said wistfully.

Behind his mask, Leopold winced. Her words were a dagger that twisted the guilt inside him.

"Then it is only fair that you indulge in your own liaison," he pronounced.

She stared at him as if contemplating his reasoning. "I—I suppose."

"What stays you?"

"Oh, I think I am not quite ready."

He advanced toward her, wanting a better look into her eyes. "What does your readiness require?"

She took a step back for every one he took towards her. "I...I know not. Well, it does not matter."

"Why?"

He was at the piano bench, and she was near the wall. He had not spoken with firm conviction when declaring that she match her husband's adultery, but he was becoming more assured that perhaps two wrongs could make a right, of sorts.

"Well, I—the pairing is surely over by now."

"Madame Follet can make arrangements. There are always the manservants. They are all handsome. You could easily avail yourself of one."

Not realizing she had come up against the wall, she

stepped backwards and bumped into it. "Oh! I think not."

He took another step toward her. She could have slid to the side and escaped his nearness, but she seemed at a loss, like a cornered mouse.

"Why not?" he demanded.

"I…"

He had drawn up before her, and she looked rather alarmed.

"Sir…"

"Why not?" he asked. The image of his wife beneath one of the rugged young bucks flashed through his mind, and he found he still balked at the notion of becoming a cuckold. But if a liaison of her own was what she desired, perhaps she deserved to have one.

"It is—they… Please."

He had closed the distance between them. As he leaned toward her, he could not keep the edge completely from his tone. "They *what?*"

She seemed to tremble. "They—they would not desire me."

He stopped.

"I am hardly a beauty," she supplied.

Unlike others of her sex, she did not reproach herself in search of compliments. She spoke with sincerity. He looked her over from head to toe. Though his wife had not the slender figure admired by most, she had a womanly suppleness to her form and other qualities to recommend her: the brightness of her eyes, the evenness of her teeth, and an unblemished

SURRENDERING TO THE BARON

complexion. He took a curl of hair and drew it before her bosom to lay upon a swollen mound.

"You underestimate your desirability, madam," he said.

She drew in a sharp breath and appeared at a loss for words.

"Perhaps," he continued, "as we are both without partners, I could oblige your purpose in coming here."

Her eyes widened, and an unexpected desire to assert his command caused heat to flow through him. How would she react if he took her into his arms right now and kissed her? Curious to know, he reached for her. Before she could object, he had wrapped his arm about her waist and drawn her to him. His mouth descended upon hers.

She gave a muffled cry and pressed her hands against his upper arms, but her resistance was weak. Her lips were softer than he remembered, and they yielded quite nicely beneath his, causing the blood in his veins to course more strongly.

He parted her lips to taste the interior of her mouth. Her stiffness began to thaw as he roamed the orifice. Her powder, rouge, and the scent of something he could not name filled his nose. When he lifted himself to allow her a breath, he could see her mind swimming. She blinked but seemed unable to focus her eyes. The flutter of her thick lashes and the heaving of her bosom called to a primal urge within him. He lowered himself to claim her mouth once more.

This startled her into motion. She slid away and

managed to stumble toward a settee in the middle of the room.

"Your offer is a kind one," she turned to say, while taking steps backward toward the egress, "but perhaps another time."

He advanced toward her. "You wound me, madam."

Her face fell. "I-I do not mean to suggest that I do not desire to be with you. It is that…"

Sweet Trudie, he thought to himself. She always did concern herself with others.

"You fear me," he filled in for her.

"I cannot say. I hardly know you. I think it is that I doubt myself."

"Doubt yourself? Permit me to show you there is no reason for it."

She hesitated, and this was all the time he required to cover the distance between them. He caught her arm and pulled her to him.

"Come," he urged. "You came to Château Follet with one intention. Let us fulfill it."

Chapter Four

H E TIGHTENED HIS GRASP on her. One hand held her arm; the other was at the small of her back, pressing her to him. Her struggles were timid, as if she feared too much resistance would be impolite.

"Is this not what you seek, my dear?" he murmured into her neck. As his lips grazed her, he felt roguish and wicked, but he could not desist. It was not merely charity or a desire to bolster her vanity that compelled his seduction. An unexpected titillation manifested in the charade he played. To his surprise, he found he wanted to possess Trudie for his own.

She gasped, leaning away from him, away from his lips. Her hands pressed against his chest, but they did little to keep him at bay. He moved his hand to her upper back. His head lowered over her chest, he kissed the small indenture at the base of her neck. Her cry turned into a groan.

His cock throbbed. Had she always felt this lush in his hands? Always smelled this enticing? Or was it the prospect that she had intended to give herself to another man that suddenly made her more alluring?

Jealousy was a common device used by women to

encourage more affection from their lovers, and he abhorred the tricks that such women employed. But Trudie had no wiles. Yet she had intended to commit adultery without his knowledge. He knew not which he preferred.

He kissed the area about her collarbone then trailed lower, to the tops of her breasts. "Come. Let us realize the intention of your journey."

She could have done more to hamper his advances—slap him, strike him, claw him—but she either knew not how or had no wish to. He did not doubt that his wife had never before found herself in such a situation, being manhandled by a stranger. She had no practice in such affairs.

Her effort to distance her bosom as far as she could from his preying mouth pushed her hips at him. He could feel her skirts surround his legs. He pressed his pelvis toward her. She leaned too far back and lost her balance. They stumbled backwards, but he guided their fall toward the settee. Now she was trapped.

He saw fear shining in her eyes—but also the glow of arousal. Blood surged through his cock.

"Please," she tried once more, like a mouse pleading to a cat for mercy.

He paused, his conscience willing him not to torment his wife. But how many men had an opportunity to ascertain the strength of their wives' fidelity? A part of him still hoped she would remain true to her marital vows, but her crimes might lessen the guilt he felt. And his seduction must surely flatter her.

He had one leg between hers, and the other knelt upon the settee against the outside of her thigh. She could not escape unless he allowed her.

"Please, what?" he inquired. "All I do is what you desire me to do."

He dropped his head and softly kissed the side of her neck. She did not fight him this time, and her dramatic breaths were not wholly the result of exertion. They held anticipation, too.

"No," she said feebly as he continued to nestle her neck. "I think—I think I erred in coming here."

"Allow me to show you that you did not."

She moaned when he put his hand upon a breast and gently slid his palm where he thought the nipple to be. He wanted the orbs bared, but her attire did not aid in his seduction. He continued to caress her neck and her décolletage till her neck arched over the back of the settee. She had a lilting pant. For the most part, she had avoided his gaze, but when he moved his hand to her ankle, she started.

"Shhh, there is naught to fear," he assured.

But her body had stiffened in alarm.

"What did your friend promise you would happen here?" he asked to distract her.

"Acts of d-depraved debauchery."

"And this appealed to you?"

"She—she said the desires of the fair sex do not differ from men, though we are taught to believe otherwise."

"Do you agree?"

She lowered her eyes farther. "I am not without lust. I suppose I am a weaker member of my sex."

He grasped her chin and lifted her gaze to his. "Desire is as natural to our bodies as hunger. You need not be ashamed. At Château Follet, these desires are exalted and fulfilled without censure. Avail yourself of the most sublime pleasure. I vow it will rival Mozart's finest concerto."

An avid admirer of that composer, she looked a little incredulous, but he was up to the task of proving his assertion.

He lowered his head to claim her mouth. She gave a muffled protest, but then her lips parted beneath his, permitting him to taste her fully. The heat in his veins flared. Her resistance had not completely dissipated, but he was glad for it, because it enabled him to apply greater pressure. With his hand upon her chin, he manipulated her so that he could sample her mouth at a variety of angles.

She inhaled sharply when he delved his tongue into her.

Despite the newness and perhaps the strangeness of having her orifice assaulted in such a manner, she sighed, barely protesting when he smothered her mouth more fully. Consumed by his kiss, she seemed not to notice his hand slipping beneath the hems of her skirts and sliding to her knee. But when his hand touched the bareness of her thigh, she yelped against his lips. She squirmed.

"I mean only to pleasure you," he murmured.

"But—"

He took her lips into his mouth, quelling her protests. Surprised to find her mouth so intoxicating, he was content to stay his hand while he kissed her long and hard. Only when he had felt her yield significantly did he move his hand to the inside of her thigh.

"Hmph," she mumbled when his hand had reached the apex and then the outset of her folds.

The devil. She was not merely damp. She was near sodden. When he nudged the flesh, she became frantic, and tried to wriggle away as if she meant to clamber over the back of the settee. He stayed her with a hand upon her shoulder.

"Calm yourself. I promise it shall not hurt."

"I am not—I am not prepared for this," she gasped.

"Prepared? My dear, this is not a concert. You have but to lie back and enjoy what I am to do."

He pressed his thumb at the nub of flesh between her folds. She cried out at the contact, her body bowing off the settee. ·

"We must not…"

Her words turned into a moan as he circled his thumb against her, slowly coaxing sensations both exquisite and torturous. Her eyes rolled toward the back of her head, and she grasped the settee as if in immense pain. He marveled at how strongly her body reacted, and when their gazes met through their masks, he glimpsed the fear he had seen in her on their wedding night. He had been too bewildered by it then to do much about it. But tonight would be different. This time he would show her the proper conclusion.

Her lips moved, but her words were lost. She squeezed her eyes shut, and it almost seemed as if she were not enjoying his fondling, but her wetness continued to flow. Her breaths grew haggard. His forefinger took a turn next, stroking that sensitive bud.

"Surrender yourself to the pleasure," he encouraged, sensing that she still fought the delicious tension. "Naught but ecstasy awaits."

His touch was still gentle. If he had been with his mistress, he would have been agitating his entire hand against her as she ground herself into him.

"Oh my, oh my," Trudie pleaded between clenched teeth.

With his fingers, he continued to build that beautiful tension from which one desired to topple. He hoped it would be so for Trudie. Her brow furrowed, and her groans and grunts increased. He sensed her arousal, but still she seemed to oppose the bliss that awaited her. He considered if his tongue might prove more effective, but such wantonness might startle her too much.

He intensified his fondling, making her legs quake. Her groans sounded slightly of sobs. Alarmed, he ceased his ministrations, but instead of looking relieved, she appeared vexed and even more distraught. She whimpered. He resumed his caresses. He would show her the end was well worth the present agitation.

Eventually, something inside her seemed to shatter, and her body went into violent paroxysm. Her cries pierced his ears as she bucked beneath him, her limbs jerking and flailing. He had never seen her spend, and was in some wonder of it. He had never seen any woman spend in such fashion, with such vigor. Desire pumped through him to the tip of his cock. The prospect of all that he could do with her filled him with excitement.

Chapter Five

WITH HER CHEEKS FLUSHED and her brow smoothed from satisfaction, Trudie looked beautiful. Her lashes fluttered, and when she opened her eyes, she gazed at him as if from a blur—but then he seemed to come into focus and she started. When Leopold bent to kiss her again, she put up her hands and tried to push him away.

"I must go," she blurted.

"We have only begun," he replied, still leaning toward her.

She pressed her hands against his chest. "No—I must."

She sounded more insistent this time, but her reservations had melted easily enough before. The swelling at his crotch grew tight at the thought of making her spend once more and in finer fashion.

"There is more pleasure, greater pleasure, to come."

She tried to slip from under him, but he, not being done with her, kept her body pinned to the sofa.

"Please," she gasped between her struggles.

Was she presently overcome with guilt? It was too late now. He reached between her legs. She tried to close them and push his hand away, but he persisted until he had reached that nub of flesh between her folds, still deliciously swollen and wet. She quivered. It was as he thought.

"No..." she moaned, but despite her protest, a radiance shone from her eyes.

With one hand, she attempted to yank his out from between her thighs while her other hand continued to push at his chest. Her squirming only caused his blood to heat further. Still wanting another kiss, he lowered his head. When her efforts gained her no traction, she shoved at his chin.

He grabbed the offending hand and pinned it to the sofa. "Do you not wish to spend again and more gloriously then before?" he asked.

"I must not." She spoke as if trying to convince herself.

He fondled her, but she became more vigorous in her struggles.

Why did she wish to stop now? Now that his member was hard as flint and yearning for release?

"I promise you an ecstasy your body has never before known," he murmured against her lips, recalling how sweet and yielding they had been.

"No! I-I have sinned enough."

Her despair ought to have stayed him, but a faint hesitation hung about her words. He felt sorry for her remorse, but if she had not wished to be unfaithful, she should never have come to Château Follet. It was true she had resisted his seduction at first, but she had eventually succumbed. And spent. She had never spent for her husband before but had done so now at the hands of a stranger, a circumstance Leopold now found vexing. A surprising jealousy flared within him.

"It is of no consequence now," he said. "You have made of your husband a cuckold already."

She slapped him across the face with her free hand, taking him by surprise. Was he the offender? After she had so willingly submitted herself?

He grabbed her second hand and crushed his mouth atop hers, muffling her scream. In her attempts to throw him off, she unwittingly pressed her body to his crotch several times, tempting the hardness there. Dispensing with his earlier tenderness, he probed her mouth roughly. The blood pounded in his head, drowning out his conscience. She was, after all, his wife. She should not be giving away what was rightfully his. As her husband, he was merely claiming his prerogative.

Her strength was no match for his. She kicked her legs, pressing her feet into the sofa to provide some leverage to free herself from beneath his weight, but his pelvis kept her pinned. He ground himself into her as his mouth continued to assault hers, his tongue probing into her moist depths. A part of him did wish to make her regret coming to the Château, but he was mostly overcome with a desire to possess her, to prove that she was his and no other's.

She twisted her head to escape his brutal kisses. Sensing she would not relent, he knew of one way to wear down her resistance. He let go of one hand and reached again between her legs.

His touch sent her into a frenzy. She pushed at his face. But the effect of his fondling was immediate, quieting her vigor.

"Please, sir," she pleaded, her protest akin to the soft mew of a kitten.

"I promise your body will know the divinest pleasure," he said, teasing and tempting the seat of her desire.

She shook her head weakly. "It is enough. Please."

But she had ceased to claw him and her body trembled beneath his. He plied her clitoris, leaving her panting anew.

"You are ready to spend again," he noted, his head swimming with the scent of her arousal.

"No."

He almost laughed at the feeble rebuff. He slid a finger into her slit. With a loud gasp, she grabbed his upper arm. The look upon her countenance called to his cock. He sank a second digit into her. She groaned. Her lashes fluttered. He curled his fingers and gently stroked.

"Dear God," she whispered, her eyes wide behind her mask, which sat askew as a result of their scuffle.

Her arousal was ripe, sensual, exciting. He wondered that he had not had the patience before to discover the beauty in her pleasure.

Trudie dug her fingers into his arm as his digits fondled her with a little more vigor. The wet heat of her quim was marvelous. Withdrawing his fingers, he straightened to undo the buttons of his fall. His member sprang free, stiff and ready. She stared at it, frightened, as if it were a weapon that could hurt her.

"I will be gent—" he began.

But she had sprung off the sofa and scrambled for the doors.

He caught her and they tumbled to the ground. She clawed and hit at him, dealing a fairly decent blow to the side of his head before he could grab her wrists and pin them to the floor.

"How unkind of you, madam. You would take pleasure but provide none in return?"

She paused briefly but resumed her resistance. Once again, her struggles only fueled the lust inside him. He had thought to prevail in his seduction, and was surprised his skills had not brought about her complete surrender. She did not understand that his cock was the superior fit for her cunnie, and that she would enjoy it much more than she had his fingers. He would show her how superb it would feel.

"Please, let me go. There are other women for you."

Recalling how easily she had dismissed herself earlier, he held her gaze in his and said, "It is you I want."

Her eyes lit up yet she continued to waver. "But…"

"Is this not what you had sought in coming here?"

She whimpered, her indecision arousing his earlier turmoil. He had a right to claim her, and his cock would be satisfied with nothing less. He wanted to show her that she was desirable. He was also cross with her for being so easily seduced by a stranger, for seeking to commit adultery. With his knee, he nudged her legs apart. He released one hand to pull up her skirts. She took the opportunity to strike at him and nearly knocked his mask off.

Stifling an oath, he flipped her onto her stomach and held her down by putting a knee to her lower back. He untied his cravat and used it to bind her wrists behind her.

"You brute!" she cried, flailing with the desperation of a fish out of water.

"You came seeking debauchery in the form of criminal congress," he reminded her. "I am merely fulfilling your intentions."

He threw her skirts over her waist, revealing plump and unblemished buttocks. If he had more patience, he would've stopped to admire them more, but his cock would wait no longer. More swiftly than he'd intended, he sank his length into her.

She gave a long cry but lay still, allowing him to savor the glory of her cunnie. He thought she would take to screaming, and he would have reconsidered his actions if she did. Instead, she whimpered.

He reached a hand around her hip, past the voluminous skirts bunched about her waist, and nestled it at her groin. His fingers found her clitoris. Her moan was long and low.

Fighting the urge to shove his entire shaft into her, he concentrated on strumming that swollen bud between her folds. She shook her head and whined a little, but he could sense her resistance melting away as more and more wetness coated his fingers. He pushed a little more of himself into her. She felt divine.

With his hand beneath her, theirs was no easy position, but he fondled her to the best of his ability. And when he had sheathed his entire cock inside her paradise, it seemed she gave a welcoming groan. He did not fault her for succumbing. There was little she could do, and a part of her must find it flattering that a man desired her enough to ravish her.

The wet heat surrounding him was irresistible, and he began a gradual thrusting. She squirmed, and he shoved deeper to keep her in place. He intensified his fondling of her clitoris.

"Oh my," she murmured.

With Trudie, it was not unlike having congress with a virgin. She was deliciously tight, and he was satisfied that it was so because no other man had spread her legs before. He was now steadily pumping in and out of her, his pelvis slapping against her rounded rump. She grunted between uneven breaths and muttered unintelligibly. It was undoubtedly an uncomfortable position for her, being pressed into the hard floor with her arms pinioned behind her and her legs spread. "Spend for me," he said.

Her grunts became cries. A few minutes later, her cries culminated in a wail, and her body fell into that familiar paroxysm. She shuddered beneath him, and it was enough to send him over the edge to join her in carnal rapture. He pulled out just as his shaft erupted, draining the tension that had built in his groin. Delicious shivers racked his body as he spent more violently than he could remember. He trembled against her till he had emptied his seed upon the floor.

When the explosion had settled into a hum in his body, he collapsed beside her to catch his breath. He closed his eyes, still in amazement at the splendor of it all.

Realizing her hands were still tied, he propped himself up and undid her bonds. She rolled onto her back and stared up at the ceiling. He took a hand and kissed it. "I pray you spent well?"

She said nothing at first, and he worried that he had been too rough with her.

"I did...thank you," she said at last.

Relieved, he lay down and looked up at the ceiling with her. Various emotions still warred within him, but he came to a decision.

He would stay a while at Château Follet after all.

Chapter Six

TRUDIE BOLTED TO HER FEET and fled the room. Seconds ago, she had lain beside a masked stranger after having had congress with him. She had even *thanked* him. What a shameful adulteress she was!

Ensconced in her own room, she sat down at the vanity, removed her mask, and peered into the looking glass, half expecting to see a changed reflection of herself. A single lamp had been left lit in the dim room, but she saw the same round face, save for the more than customary crimson flush, staring back at her. Committing adultery had not transformed her into an ugly monster.

Rather, the blush in her cheeks became her, and even the disarray of her coiffure was not without a bucolic charm. A man had found her enticing enough to seduce. She could not deny that it had been thrilling. More than thrilling. Unimaginable. She had spent – not once, but twice. And it had been glorious, the most exquisite sensation her body had ever known. But such bliss had occurred at the hand of a stranger. How could it be, when she had not ever done so with her own husband before, a man whom she loved and found more than alluring?

She felt her flush deepen as she recalled how her body had succumbed. It had betrayed her better judgment. He had been inside her, his fingers, his…shaft. Inside her most private parts. The penetration had hurt at first, though not nearly as bad as it had upon her marriage night. Tonight, for a few minutes, she had wished to be anywhere but pinned beneath him, speared upon his stiff erection. But then the arousal took over. She was no match for the more primitive carnal desires. The sensations that followed were the most delicious she had ever known. The evidence of the rapture still clung to her thighs.

Now came the remorse. The shame. How could she have done what she had? It was a mistake to come here to Château Follet. She should never have allowed her friend, Diana, to talk her into coming. She should flee, return home and contemplate the sin she had committed. Despite the late hour, she stood and began to pack her belongings.

"Whatever are you doing?"

Trudie looked up to see her husband's beautiful cousin. Diana had been in the company of a flaxen haired Adonis earlier, unabashedly flirting with him.

"I cannot stay," Trudie replied.

Diana raised a single brow. "I thought we had discussed the matter. You owe your husband nothing. Leopold broke his vows first."

"Two wrongs do not make a right."

"No, they do not, but they make an *equivalency*, and

it is not unfair to pay a wrong with a wrong."

"I cannot perceive it to be so. I feel far too wretched!"

"But why? Your being here... oh! What has happened?" Diana approached the bed where Trudie had placed her portmanteau.

Trudie began to tremble. "I met a man."

Diana's eyes lit up. "Truly! That is wonderful! Who is it?"

"I do not even know his name, which makes it all the more awful," Trudie groaned.

"Not at all. In fact, it is much better that way. You need not worry of ever crossing paths with him. But you must tell me more! Was he handsome?"

"I could not tell. He wore a mask. I do not care if he was handsome or not. I wish it had not happened."

"Don't be such a silly ninny. Did he—you—both—"

"I do not think I can speak of it."

"And here I had come expecting to find you bored out of your mind. This is wondrous! You ought to take pride in your liaison. Our husbands, Leopold and Charles, have had their mistresses for some time. Now it is our turn to have a little merriment. Where is your mystery lover now? Why is he not with you?"

"I neither know nor care. I fled from him and hope to depart the château as soon as possible."

Diana put her hands on her hips. "And where do you expect to go? Considering the lateness of the hour, you cannot leave."

Realizing this to be true, Trudie sank down onto the bed. A numbness crept into her. She did not think she could wait till morning to make arrangements, but she saw little alternative.

Diana threw her arms about Trudie. "I am so happy for you, my dear! If I were you, I would seek out your mystery lover. Why spend the night alone?"

Trudie shook her head vehemently. "He is the last person I wish to see at present."

"Well, I am sorry to hear it and hope you will change your mind. I must not keep my gentleman waiting or he will be cross with me."

With a final embrace, Diana took her leave. Still feeling miserable, Trudie stared at the wall before her. What was she to do now? What would she do when she returned home? When she faced Leopold?

"What a wretch am I," she grumbled to herself, putting her head into her hands. "I must pay a proper penance for my deeds."

"That can be arranged."

Trudie leaped off the bed and whipped around. It was *him*.

* * * * *

Her heart jumped into her throat at seeing the source of her debauchery, his tall form filling the doorway. He still wore his mask, and she realized she did not have hers. The odds that he knew her were slim, but she was tempted to grab for her mask, which, alas, lay out of arm's reach. Moreover, her feet were frozen to their spot though every nerve urged her to flee.

"You left without a by your leave," he said in a stern tone.

She found it difficult to swallow.

"Did I err in judgment?" he asked more gently. "Did you not spend in pleasure?"

Her legs began to quiver. She told herself she ought not fear this man as much as she did. She sensed that he was capable of gentleness, but he had manhandled her forcefully and without apparent qualm.

Finding her voice at last, she said, "If I did, it was an error."

"Error? How can that be? Did you not enjoy it?"

"Yes, but – I mean, no. I ought not have. It was wrong."

"And all the more tantalizing for that reason." He pressed his lips together into a line as if vexed with her.

"In the moment perhaps. But it was wrong and not worth the consequences."

His countenance lightened. "You wound me, madam."

He advanced a step into the room. She immediately took a step back. "Your pardon, sir. It is only – I am married."

Tears pressed against the back of her eyes.

"As am I."

Her eyes widened at what he had said. She saw no wedding ring upon his hand.

Seeing her gaze, he answered, "My ring is safe in my

bedchamber. It is far more effective if I do not wear it here at Château Follet."

"You may be at ease with being an adulterer, but I am not."

He stiffened. "Did you not say that your husband had already broken his vows?"

"Yes, but it is different for a husband."

"Why?"

"What do you mean?"

"Is it not hypocritical to expect a wife to be faithful when her husband is not?"

"It is different for a man."

"You expect that women should adhere to higher standards and deny themselves the same pleasures that men avail themselves of?"

"You sound very much like my friend."

"Perhaps your friend has the more enlightened view."

Trudie looked down in consideration. She wanted to believe what Diana and he said. But it was difficult.

"I think some allowances must be made for husbands who have been compelled to marry wives who are not so captivating."

"You think your husband does not find you captivating?"

She met his gaze. "I'm certain of it."

"I beg to differ. You are more than captivating."

"I am no woman of great accomplishment —"

"You are an accomplished pianist."

"My sole talent. I am not otherwise accomplished. I

do not dance elegantly, I do not converse with wit and cleverness, I do not –"

"You spend beautifully."

Her pulse quickened. Once more warmth grew inside her body. But she ought not give in to such temptations. She ought not give in to his seductive ways.

"I have committed a terrible sin. I bid you take your leave, sir, that I may contemplate my wrong in solitude."

"What of your penance? What shall you do?"

"I know not, but I would do anything to make it right."

To her horror, he closed and locked the doors behind him. "What – what do you do, sir?" She had been lulled into comfort during their dialogue, but comfort with him was misplaced.

"Finding a way to make it right. Perhaps penance can be arranged."

* * * * *

Her mind reeled.

He continued to advance into the room. "You have been a naughty little miss, have you not?"

She backed away. What did he intend to do?

As if sensing her fear, he said, "Worry not. You will thank me at the end—as you had done before."

She was aghast. Thank him? For what? "I asked you to leave, sir," she said, her mouth turning dry.

"You do not have the privilege of issuing commands here."

"I beg you to consider the request of a lady."

"Are you a 'lady'?" he challenged, coming around the bed. "Would a 'lady' be wet with desire between her legs?"

She flushed. The area between her thighs pulsed. Dear God, it was happening again. She backed away from him, but he had her cornered once more. Behind her: a wall. To her left: a wall. To her right: the bed. And in front of her: him, standing but a foot from her.

"I think a proper education in the carnal arts is all you need."

"What you contemplate is wrong," she murmured..

"It is what you came to Château Follet for," he reminded her.

There was no reasoning with him. Her best chance was to escape. When he reached for her, she dove toward the bed and tried to scramble over the top of it. He caught her and once again she found herself trapped beneath him. When she attempted to push him off of her, he grabbed her wrists and pinned them to the bed.

"I see you favor playing the damsel in distress," he remarked.

She could feel his breath and caught a glint in his eyes through his mask. She started. There was something familiar about his eyes.

"You need not fear," he continued. "You will take pleasure in all that I do to you."

She shook her head, not wanting to believe it possible.

"I shall scream," she warned.

"Screams are commonplace here, but if you truly wish for me to go, I shall."

When she hesitated, his mouth descended onto hers. His lips captured hers, muffling her protests and blurring her thoughts. She could not think clearly when kissed by him. Her mind fought to surface above the currents that waved through her body and seemed to collect between her thighs. How was it possible she could enjoy this, enjoy being surrounded by his strength, restrained against her will? Because this man, unlike Leopold, desired her. This stranger was the only man to desire her. The warmth inside her grew as his mouth coaxed hers to open. His tongue met hers, teasing and wanton. Closing her eyes, she gave in to the lovely assault, allowing him to delve and probe every recess of her mouth.

No, no. She ought to resist. She should not permit herself to be so pathetic as to allow the stranger to seduce her a second time. Though she knew it to be futile, she struggled against him. In response, his hips pressed her further into the bed. The kiss became both a duel and a dance as she wavered between resisting and surrendering. His mouth pressed harder, rougher, and to her surprise, the intensity only added to the thrill. He kissed her long and hard till she grew breathless, till her jaw was sore, and her resistance wearied. When, at long last, he separated his mouth from hers, she could form no words above her panting.

He gazed into her eyes. "Much better. Now, if you do as I bid and please me, I shall have no cause to set to lecturing you. Indeed, I may have cause to reward you if you are obedient."

Obedient? Did he speak to her as if he meant to train a pet dog?

Grabbing her, he pulled her off the bed. He transferred both her wrists to one hand while his other hand yanked off the sash that held the bed curtains in place. He used the sash to bind her wrists together.

Panic formed anew in her throat. "What do you intend?"

He pulled her onto her feet and toward one of the bedposts. He pulled off another sash and used it to tie her wrists to the bedpost. "Please," she pleaded.

"Did you not say you wish to pay penance for your deeds?" he asked, crooking a finger and running the knuckle along her décolletage. His fingers skimmed the tops of her breasts. "Did you not say that you would do anything to set it right?"

"But how is this to serve such purposes?"

"You shall see."

What came next dismayed her greatly. He circled his arms about her and began to feel for and remove the pins that held her dress together. He meant to undress her!

"No... Please..." She prayed he did not intend to reveal her form. How she wished she had Diana's slenderness or a body worth exposing, any body but hers. Without the pins, her bodice loosened. Realizing the sleeves still encased her arms he gripped the fabric and tore it. The garment slid off her shoulder.

"Dear God," she whimpered.

He did the same to the other sleeve. The top of her dress slid to the floor, leaving her arms bare, her corset revealed. Her ample breasts swelled high above the undergarment. He stood to admire them before lowering his head to kiss them.

"Captivating," he said after he had raised his head. His tone made her shiver. He untied her skirts and petticoats next. She watched in dread as he pulled these down to the floor. She could only hope that he would go no further.

He cupped the side of her face and traced her bottom lip with his thumb. It was a gentle caress that caused her heart to palpitate as much as his rougher movements. He replaced his thumb with a finger, which edged closer and closer into her mouth. She took in his digit as if it were the most natural and obvious thing to do. She tongued his finger and sucked. When she dared to meet his gaze, the look of lust smoldering in his eyes beckoned her own arousal.

"Well, well," he murmured, "I think we may make a wanton of you yet."

Chapter Seven

S HE BALKED. SURELY HE jested. She was a good girl. She had always been a proper and decent young woman.

Yet, she could not deny that she had willingly taken his digit into her mouth and sucked it readily. She had come to Château Follet to indulge in criminal carnality. She was now an adulteress. Was she not a wanton jade already?

As if sensing her pain, he added gently, "Worry not. You will enjoy every minute of it."

She looked at him with defiance. She may have committed a wrong, gone down the devil's path, but she need not worsen her guilt.

"My friend will return at any moment," she warned.

He leaned in closer, and she could feel his heat, smell his essence. It was vaguely familiar.

"A nice attempt," he whispered, "but your friend is in the embrace of a compelling fellow. I doubt she will return. She is a woman given to indulging her passions and has not your reservations."

She struggled to find a threat that would affect him, finally deciding on, "I shall tell Madame Follet of your behavior. She will not condone it. She may ban you from her château."

He kissed her gently beneath the ear, making her shiver. With his lips, he continued to softly caress her neck.

"Perhaps not," he agreed, "but it will be worth the exile if I can have my way with you this night."

She tried to suppress her groan. Her legs weakened. Leopold had never said such things to her, and as she was one who rarely engendered compliments, she had to admit that her starvation for attention lent greater potency to his words.

"I suggest you follow in your friend's footsteps," he said, now mouthing her throat, "for that is what you had intended all along."

But I had intended not to see it through, she thought to herself, *until you came along.* But there was no use in placing blame. She was not faultless and had been a willing party to her own demise.

His lips seared the soft spot beneath her jaw, draining her resistance. How was it she could be so easily seduced by this man? Was it so easy for her to succumb to any man willing to desire her, or was it this man in particular who held sway over her?

His arm reached behind her and began to untie her skirts.

I must not allow this. She resorted to bribery. "Sir, if you will desist, I can offer you ten pounds—"

He snorted.

"Fifty pounds, then."

"Does your husband allow you that much pin

money?"

His kisses now trailed down to her décolletage, and she could not stay her bosom from heaving.

"I have my own funds. My family is one of means. It is the reason my husband married me."

He stiffened. "That cannot be the sole reason."

"That and our families have long been well acquainted."

He straightened. He cupped her chin and tilted her gaze up to meet his. His eyes bore into hers. "You could offer me a hundred pounds. I will not forgo you, my dear."

She could not breathe. She supposed he must be well situated himself for monetary reward to have such little consequence upon him. But what if he were not?

He pulled down her skirt, along with her petticoats, which he had apparently untied as well. She stood before him in nothing but her undergarments: her chemise, corset, stockings and garters. She began to wonder that she could survive the night with this man. Without her gown, her form was exposed to him. She tried not to think how he would assess her wide hips and plump thighs. But he dismissed her thoughts when he took her mouth in his. His hand cupped the back of her head, trapping her, so that he could devour her. The pressure of his lips roving over hers made her head spin. He pried her lips open, and his tongue was deep in her orifice, licking, caressing, probing. He kissed her with greater intensity than he had in the piano room. She could not keep pace with the assault. Yet, she found herself wishing that Leopold would kiss her in such fashion. When at long last he gave her a reprieve, her jaw was sore and her lips bruised. She was breathless. And warm. Extremely warm.

His free hand rested on her left hip before brushing across her thigh toward her mound. She began to struggle. If he should fondle her *there*, the odds would multiply against her. As she feared he would, he cupped her between the legs, pressing the fabric of her chemise into her dampness, making her quiver. She should speak the word of safety. She gave a half-hearted attempt, but the word was muffled by his lips atop hers. His fingers curled against her folds through the chemise.

"You wished to speak, madam?" he murmured against her mouth. He was breathless, too.

Heart hammering, she only managed a moan. He was stroking her, coaxing more moisture to her most intimate parts. Her mind commanded her to object. But the area between her legs spoke louder. The sensations fluttering from her nether regions were more delicious, more tempting than the finest of wines.

When she made no further sound, he took her mouth again, his lips enveloping hers, drowning her with his passion. Her arousal surged in response. She found herself grinding into his hand, seeking that euphoric end she had experienced in the piano room.

But he withdrew, leaving her bereft, her body groaning at the loss of his touch.

Sauntering behind her, he sat at the corner of the bed and reached for the ribbons of her corset. The garment would be his next victim. The thought of being completely naked before him, her rounded body exposed, jolted her to some semblance of order. She tried to take this opportunity to collect her wits and consider a plan of escape. Without the vision of him before her to distract her, she might actually be able to think. But still it was no easy task. The force of his kisses still burned her lips. She had appealed, threatened, and bribed him. What else could she do?

With her wrists bound atop her head to the bedpost, he could not remove the corset, nor could he tear through its whalebone as he had with the silk bodice of her gown. Aware of this, he untied the sash from the bedpost after he had loosened her corset. As soon as her arms came down, she attempted to wrestle away from him. Her wrists were still bound by the initial sash, and he used that to yank her back to him. She fell across his lap, grazing the hardness between his legs.

"Behave yourself," he said gruffly, "or you may not like the consequences."

"What do you mean?" she asked.

In answer, he threw the chemise over her backside, baring her rump. She felt her cheeks turn red. A more embarrassing predicament could not be had.

Whack!

She yelped at the sting of his hand against a buttock. Horror filled her as he dealt another blow. She was being spanked! She had been spanked only once before in her life when, at six years of age, she had stolen her younger brother's biscuits and eaten them all.

But to be spanked as a grown woman! This was highly objectionable—*more than* objectionable!

She was about to protest when a third and even harder smack was delivered. She gave a cry of anguish. Damn his insolence! How dare he?

"Sir! I am a baroness." She attempted to speak with hauteur to make herself more impressive. "And—and I'll not suffer such treatment!"

"You may claim to be a duchess. Your treatment would not differ here at Château Follet."

He emphasized his words with another wallop to her other buttock. It seemed as if little needles poked at her derriere, but the pain was easily tolerated. The humiliation was the harder aspect to bear.

"Stop!" she cried after another spank.

To her surprise, he did. But only to let his hand wander beneath her rump and between her legs. He caressed her folds, the bud between. She whimpered. The sweetness of his touch contrasted with the burn upon her backside, a unique pairing that confused and intrigued.

When he smacked her again, she made no protest, hoping instead that he would fondle her, which he did. He alternated between pleasuring her and punishing her.

"Do you still wish me to desist?" he inquired after her arse felt as if it were on fire.

She stared at the bedclothes beneath them, glad he could not see her face. She was sure her countenance blushed as crimson as her derriere. Despite the assault upon her backside, her desire had not diminished in the least. Rather, it had grown.

Slowly, she shook her head. Perhaps she was, as he had mentioned, a wanton.

* * * * *

To her disappointment, he neither resumed his caresses nor spanked her. He undid the binding at her wrists, then lifted her. Her arms came out of the sleeves of the corset. She felt her breasts, which had been pushed up toward her collar, drop. He flipped her onto her back and straddled her.

"Please, let me keep the chemise," she asked, unable to bear the thought of being completely naked before him.

"Will you behave?" he replied.

She nodded, searching for his eyes through his mask to find some assurance that he was not all ruthlessness. When his mouth seared the side of her neck, she ceased to care. She wanted him to address the agitation humming in her loins. He planted kisses all across her bosom before pulling down the chemise to bare a breast. Cupping it, he gazed upon the orb with reverence. He planted light kisses upon the mound, upon the large areola, then took her already erect nipple into his mouth. She shivered and closed her eyes. Leopold had done something similar their wedding night, and she had nearly leapt from her own skin. Though small, the nipple exuded an astronomical amount of sensation. She could hardly stand it. It was too much.

She tried to push his head away. He had begun licking the rosy bud, sending reverberations through her whole body, making her toes curl.

"Enough!" she gasped, trying to turn her body away.

But he had a firm grip upon her breast. "Behave if you wish to keep your chemise."

She whimpered and tried to still her body, tried not to heed the assault upon her defenseless nipple. But when he began sucking, albeit slightly, she did not think she could stand it any longer. Once more she tried to push his head off of her and nearly knocked his mask askew. This seemed to make him cross. He flipped her over and retied her wrists behind her before turning her back over. He adjusted his mask.

"You shall pay for your disobedience, madam."

Grabbing the neckline of her chemise, he tore the garment down the middle. She sobbed as her body lay exposed to him. She could not look at him, not when he could see all of her — her rounded hips, the swell of her belly, the ampleness of her thighs. Tears pressed against her eyes. She desperately wished to be anywhere but here.

She felt his hand lightly caressing her curves. His touch felt tender, almost as if he appreciated rather than abhorred the flesh.

I deserve this, she thought to herself. This mortifying embarrassment was her penance for the wrong she had committed. She lay in silent submission, unable to speak or move while his hands wandered all over her.

His mouth was over her nipple once more, and she gave a cry. She clenched her teeth when he sucked harder. It was oddly pleasing in small part but mostly torturous. One hand of his was between her thighs, stroking her, and this helped to alleviate a little of the discomfort of his sucking. She squirmed beneath him as he intensified his actions upon both areas. She could not tell which was greater: the delicious waves spreading from that other rosebud or the acute discomfort upon her nipple.

The latter won out when he bit her nipple. She gave a shriek.

"Please..." she begged.

The other words were lost in her throat for he had intensified his fondling. It was the strangest of delights, this agitation that both vexed and pleased, an agitation that left one worse off in its absence. She wanted that euphoric end, that pinnacle of tension that would leave her satiated and calm after the storm. And it seemed he would provide it to her, but he began nibbling on her nipple, occasionally nipping her flesh. Her body pressed into the mattress, as if she could sink into it and escape the ravaging of his mouth. The lower half of her body sought the opposite, seeking his hand when it drifted higher. She gasped in both pleasure and pain, groaned in agony and moaned in delight.

He slowed the ministrations between her legs and gradually came off her nipple. Her body was in a state of confusion. She panted heavily, and a tear slid from an eye. She quivered at the loss of sensation. She was relieved not to have his attention to her nipple, but that other part of her throbbed in need. Though wanting to know his thoughts, she dared not gaze at him.

"Do you wish me to continue?" he inquired.

She did not know. She could not stand his nips, but her body craved his fondling. He waited patiently for her response.

"Yes," she said meekly, then wondered if she had gone mad.

He held her other breast and licked the nipple. She began to regret her decision almost immediately. He swirled his tongue and coaxed the nipple to full hardness. She trembled at what was to come, but he eased her fears when he resumed stroking her between the legs. She yelped when he nipped the nipple with his teeth, but he rewarded her with more of his beautiful caresses, lifting her body towards the heavens of carnal rapture. With his attentions, her body climbed toward that longed-for precipice, but whenever she came near to going over its edge, he lightened his touch and bit down harder upon her nipple. It was a slow and arduous dance between pain and pleasure. Her body felt stretched to its limits. To her dismay, he groped both breasts, pushed them together, and alternated between the two nipples, kissing, roughly sucking, biting. Her body wanted to curl into itself like a snail into its shell. She screamed and sobbed. The word of safety was upon her lips when he stopped. He slid down her body and situated himself between her thighs. He tongued that nub of pleasure, making her want to scramble toward the ceiling. Her nipples still smarted, but there was no ignoring that blissful heat in her groin. He licked quickly but skillfully and deliberately. Soon the waves of pleasure melded with the soreness of her nipples. She could not sustain the storm raging inside her body. She felt herself catapulted into a sea of ecstasy. Her body convulsed violently, but he held her in place as his tongue continued its wicked, wanton assault. Her body shattered into pieces, each one shaking to its own tune, and she wondered that she could ever be put back together.

Chapter Eight

A S LEOPOLD SPENCER BEHELD his wife lying upon the bed, her body bared to him, he was struck by how beautiful she looked. Her chemise hung in tatters at her sides. Her arms, still pinioned beneath her, caused her breasts to thrust outward. Beautiful breasts with large areolas that seemed to occupy half the mounds even whilst her nipples stood hardened. He had assaulted those elongated rosebuds with much pleasure. At times her shrieks and sobs had made him wonder if he had gone too far, but she had not commanded him to leave.

He had overheard Trudie's conversation with his cousin Diana.

"Leopold broke his vows first," Diana had said

"Two wrongs do not make a right," Trudie had replied.

"No, they do not, but they make an equivalency, and it is not unfair to pay a wrong with a wrong."

Leopold could not disagree with Diana, but still he was not happy that Trudie had come to Château Follet. The wicked debauchery that occurred here was not for Trudie.

Or so he had thought.

Another tear glistened in the corner of her eye, and between her legs glistened the moisture of her desire. Heat swirled in his body, and the stiffness of his cock was more than uncomfortable. But he was not done with Trudie. He had brought her to spend, which was more than she deserved. But he also felt sorry for her, had received her earlier statements about him with sorrow. He had not been a good husband, he realized. He was at best a decent one for he did not treat her poorly. But he had neglected her because, in truth, as she suspected, he had not been fully captivated by her. Taking her regard for him for granted, he knew he could have chosen for himself a prettier wife, a wittier one. Her boldness in coming to Château Follet had thus surprised him. Perhaps he did not know Trudie as well as he had thought.

Holding himself over her, he brushed his lips softly over hers. She sighed against his mouth. Gently, he kissed her and tried not to think on how she gave of herself to a stranger.

Reaching beneath, he cupped a breast, weighed the heaviness in his hand. She whimpered, then gasped and grunted when he rolled the nipple between thumb and forefinger. She squirmed. Her body was exceedingly sensitive, he recalled of their wedding night and how everything he did seemed to make her leap out of her own skin. Her reactions had him taken aback. They had consummated the marriage but not without tears and much distress on her part. He had made few attempts with her after that.

But the experience of Château Follet had proved quite different. She had spent, thrice now, at the hands of a stranger. His mask hid his identity from her, as she probably thought hers did from him. He tugged at her nipple, and with some anger, pinched it. She cried out. He slapped the side of her breast, making it wobble. He slapped the other orb. Her breasts were too beautiful not to ravish. Climbing atop the bed, he straddled her ribs. He unbuttoned his fall and released his shaft. She stared at it with widened eyes. No doubt she had never seen a man's member this close before. He rubbed his arousal and tugged it before laying it between her breasts. He squeezed them together till they encased him with their warm suppleness. Slowly thrusting his hips, he slid his rod between her flesh. She watched in bewilderment—or perhaps amazement.

His seed soon spilled over her bosom and coated the area of her collarbone. He had thought to resist. The crude wantonness of spending upon her might horrify Trudie. But the loveliness of her breasts, the thought of marking her with his mettle, proved too enticing.

A drop had landed near a corner of her lips. Feeling wicked, he brushed it with his thumb into her mouth. The distinctive tang made her grimace. She coughed a little when he pressed his thumb onto her tongue.

He was going to go to hell.

Never would he have thought to find himself doing what he did to his wife, but she had engendered in him a mix of emotions in coming to Château Follet. It was wrong but intoxicating to see her both helpless and aroused.

Withdrawing himself, he climbed off of her. Her expression held some misery, and he felt a little ashamed once more. But he was seeing a whole new side of Trudie, one that greatly intrigued him. He wanted to know how far this dark and mysterious part of her extended, for her dismay at being undressed and tied up had not prevented her arousal. For the third time tonight, she had spent—and at the hand, shaft and tongue of a man she believed a stranger to her.

His vexation of her unfaithfulness had not completely dissipated, though he accepted that he had played a part, albeit not purposefully, in compelling her to seek a place such as the Château Debauchery. He recognized the hypocrisy of his anger—he had broken the marital vows first and had entertained a mistress for some time—but more was simply expected in the wife. Nevertheless, had he been a more attentive husband, he doubted Trudie would have ventured here.

At first, he had wanted to challenge her fidelity, then, out of pity, he had decided to grant her the debauchery she had sought, to provide her the thrill she lacked in her marriage. He had not expected the situation to arouse his own desires as much as it did. Trudie was not the plain simpleton he had once thought her. He found himself eager to take her to the world of wanton carnal pleasure.

Replacing his fall, he said, "Let us now continue with your lesson."

* * * * *

Rolling her onto her stomach, he undid the bindings at her wrists, then shed her tattered undergarments. She was now naked, completely naked, save for her stockings and garters.

"Stand," he commanded.

With lowered lashes, she did as he bid. His mettle, adorning her collar, had begun to dry, but a bit of it slid down toward her breasts. He could have wiped it away but decided to leave his mark upon her to remind her that she was his.

She covered herself with her arms and hands, still clearly uncomfortable baring her body to him.

"No, you must not cover yourself. It pleases me to see all of you."

Reluctantly, she lowered her arms to her sides. He circled about her, taking in her body at differing angles. Unlike his slender mistress, his wife possessed a full body. What he had hitherto deemed plump, he now found rather lush. Her rounded hips and thighs had a simple quality, her large breasts were ripe for delicious torment.

"While I do not disagree that penance is in order, I think a proper lesson might prove the better solution. Perhaps you would like to learn how to please your husband?"

She said nothing but seemed to consider his suggestion.

"Here at Château Follet, I shall be your master," he

declared, "and you are my student and wench. Is that understood?" When she made no answer, he repeated, "Do you understand?"

"Yes, sir," she said in a small voice.

He was pleased with the proper respect that she was voicing to him, but he said, "Louder."

"Yes, sir."

"Good. Restate the roles for me."

"Sir?"

"What is my role here?"

She refrained from looking him in the eye. "You are the master."

"And what are you?"

"Your student."

"And?"

She squirmed before responding, "Your wench."

"And why are you my wench?" he asked as he continued to saunter around her. He eyed her arse, which he had spanked earlier. He would have to attend it more.

"I hardly know."

"Is it because you stand stripped to the buff before a man?"

"I suppose."

"Is it because you came here seeking debauchery?"

She nodded.

"Answer me."

"Yes, sir."

"Is it because you have allowed a man you know not to touch you, to fondle you?"

"Yes, sir."

"Is it because you have spent at the hands of a stranger?"

"Yes, sir."

"Is it because you commit adultery with ease?"

Her head snapped up and she met his gaze. Her eyes held emotion he could not place.

"For which you are now being schooled," he provided.

"Yes, sir."

Her voice shook, and he thought she might cry. She lowered her head. Cupping her chin, he lifted her gaze to meet his. "Worry not. I shall return you to your husband a better woman."

Her eyes widened.

"You do not think it possible? Tell me, how do you pleasure your husband?"

"He does not seek pleasure from me."

"And if he did? How would you provide it?"

"I know not. I am not versed in such matters. I imagine it a significant reason for why he has himself a mistress."

"Would you like to be well versed in pleasuring your husband?"

She nodded.

"Would you like to be more proficient than his mistress?"

Her eagerness was writ upon her face.

"I promise you, by the end of the evening, you will know precisely how to please your husband. We will begin by caressing your body." He went to stand behind her and placed a hand upon her shoulder. He heard a hitch in her breath. He slid his hand down her arm. "You must not be ashamed of your body."

He grazed the back of two fingers along her hip, up her waist, and toward her breast.

"I cannot pretend I am a beauty when I am not," she resisted.

"Shhh. Do only as I say. Touch yourself."

She only stood awkwardly.

"Touch yourself," he said again.

"Where?"

"'Where, *sir*.'"

"Where, sir?"

"The breasts. They are fine assets of yours."

She placed her hand over the orbs.

"Now caress them."

She gave herself a pat. He almost laughed at the chasteness. "More. Worship them with your hands."

Again she stood immobile and awkward.

"Squeeze them."

She gave her breasts a squeeze.

With a shake of the head, he reached around her. "Like this."

He cupped both breasts and gave the mounds a lascivious press. He kneaded the fullness of her flesh.

"They are exquisite, are they not?" he murmured as warmth percolated in his loins. "Answer me."

"Yes, sir."

"Your turn." He withdrew his hands and went to

stand in front of her to watch her replicate his motions. "Sink your fingers into them, feel their suppleness and exalt in their grandness. Now play with the nipples."

She hesitated, and he suspected the buds were still sore from his prior attentions.

"If you do not attend them, I will," he threatened.

She placed a forefinger over one nipple and flicked it gently. She shivered.

"Now pinch them."

After a pause, she pinched the nipple.

"Good. Now pull the succulent little bud."

She did a quick tug.

"Harder."

She tugged again, groping herself, pressing and rolling the mounds over her chest.

"I assure you that your husband would witness this with great pleasure. Don't forget the nipples."

This time she gave them a proper tug.

"Very good. Now lick them."

"Sir?"

Her breasts were large and malleable enough that she could do it. To assist her, he cupped the bottom of a breast and pushed it upward. With his other hand he pushed her head down toward the waiting nipple.

"Lick," he commanded.

Her tongue emerged and gave a tentative lick.

"More."

Heat traveled to his head. She gave herself two more licks.

"Now take it into your mouth."

His cock throbbed as he watched her enclose her mouth over her nipple.

"Suck it."

More of her rosy areola disappeared into her mouth. The urge to ravish her came on sudden and strong, but he held himself in check.

"Now the other," he directed.

On her own, she pushed her other breast up to her mouth. After giving the nipple a few licks, she took it into her mouth and sucked.

"Well done. Now you may play with your quim."

She balked.

"Does it disconcert you to fondle yourself before a stranger?"

"Of course."

"Do you find it lewd, wanton?"

She nodded.

"Humiliating?"

She bit her bottom lip and nodded again.

"Then this shall be both pleasure and penance. You may sit upon the bed if you wish."

She went to the bed and sat down but did not touch yourself.

"Spread your legs, my dear."

When she hesitated still, he went over and reached for her nipple. Immediately, she spread her legs. He took her right hand and placed it at her mons.

"Show me how you pleasure yourself."

"I do not," she murmured.

He lifted his brows. "You do not bring yourself

pleasure? Not even in the privacy of your bedchamber?"

She shook her head.

"You have not touched yourself there?"

"On occasion…but I do not bring myself to spend."

"Why not?"

"I was afraid to."

"Afraid? But why?"

She knit her brows in thought. "I feared doing so would overwhelm me."

"But you spent tonight—more than once."

She looked up at him. "It was forced upon me."

He returned a wry smile. "Not entirely, madam."

She looked down once more. She must know she had played no small part in what had transpired.

"Do you mean to tell me that you had never spent till now?" he inquired.

She nodded without meeting his gaze. He was silent in disbelief. He knew his wife to be uncomfortable with him in bed, but he had assumed she at least knew how to pleasure herself.

"Then this is an occasion worth celebrating," he said at last.

"Celebrate a sin?" she replied with dismay.

"You enjoyed spending, did you not?" he asked, approaching her.

At his nearness, she sat at attention.

Hoping to jolt her out of her guilt and remorse, he said in a stern tone, "Answer me."

She gave a tentative nod.

"With words."

"I did."

"And do you wish to spend again?"

"No…or, perhaps…"

"Yes or no?"

"Yes."

"Louder."

"Yes, sir."

"Then touch yourself."

She hesitated.

"There will be a price to pay if you do not follow my directions promptly."

At that, she placed her hand between her thighs.

"Now stroke yourself."

Timidly, she grazed her middle finger along her folds.

Crossing his arms, he stood directly in front of her. "Spread your legs wider."

She followed his directive less tentatively this time. The area of his groin tightened to see the supple lips of her cunnie.

"Do you feel that nub in the center?"

"Yes."

"Do you know what it is called?"

"No, sir."

"The clitoris. Do you know it has no bodily function but that of generating pleasure? Its nature is purely carnal. It enjoys being touched, does it not?"

"I suppose."

"You suppose? Then you must attend it more

properly."

Stepping toward her, he pushed her hand more forcefully into her flesh. She gasped.

"Stroke yourself in earnest," he directed.

"But... this – this ought to be a private act."

"This what?"

"This touching of oneself."

"There is a name for such an act. Do you know what it is?"

She flushed.

"You know the word. Say it."

She blushed even deeper, and he could not resist triumphing a little in her discomfort.

"You make me wait too often, my dear," he warned.

"M—Masturbation," she mumbled.

"You allowed me to touch you there earlier. How is this different?"

"Because it is. Because you're standing there, doing nothing but watching."

He grinned. "It distresses you?"

"To say the least!"

He chuckled. "Then let us do it together. If it will ease your distress to know that I too have employment."

He unbuttoned his fall and pulled out his stiff erection. She glanced away in modesty at first but then stole several glances at his cock. He rubbed himself until his shaft was at full length. She was now staring at it, taking in the flare of the head and the ridges of the shaft.

"You will fondle yourself, and I will do the same," he said. "Now, my dear."

Her lashes fluttered but she resumed stroking herself.

"That is not so hard, is it?" he inquired. "Does your clitoris not enjoy your petting?"

Her brow furrowed. Her caresses had become more purposeful.

"Answer me."

"Yes," she murmured.

"Address me properly."

"Yes, sir."

"Good. Have you noticed how swollen it is? It wants more of your touch. It is a greedy, wanton little bud. We must attend its need, its purpose. For our efforts, it will return that most divine of carnal bliss."

"I could not—I have never—"

"But you shall. We shall not stop until you do."

She frowned in worry.

"Lie back and close your eyes," he advised, "but continue your caresses."

She did as he bid.

"Now with your other hand, you will take a breast and squeeze it, caress it, exalt in the lushness of your flesh."

His cock was hard as flint as he watched her naked form displayed upon the bed, one hand of hers upon the breast, the other between her legs.

"But how naughty of you to be touching yourself in such fashion."

Her eyes flew open. "But you told me—"

He smiled. "And how naughty of you to enjoy it. But you are a naughty little wench are you not, Tru—truly?"

He had nearly spoken her name.

"For only the naughtiest of wenches would come to a place like the Château Follett," he continued. "Only sluts would spend for a man not their husband."

She whimpered. He should have refrained from making such a statement. He had to be careful for he did not want her guilt to interfere with her arousal.

"Tell me you are a naughty wench."

"I am a naughty wench."

"Louder."

"I am a naughty wench!"

Her fingers quickened against herself.

"Tell me you are a wanton."

"I am a wanton."

"Now make yourself spend."

She agitated her fingers fiercely against her clitoris.

"Are you close to spending, my dear?"

"Yes, sir."

"Then look at me. I want to see into your eyes when you spend."

She gazed at him but soon lost focus as her arousal climbed toward its peak. Her mouth fell open. Her brows knit. Her back arched. Then came the spasms, the trembles of her body falling over the precipice. A soft cry accompanied the paroxysm.

"That, my dear, was a beautiful sight," he said after

the last of the quivering had left her body and she had relaxed into the bed. He stroked his hardened desire. "And now you will attend my arousal."

* * * * *

"You should appear more eager, my dear," he said of her slight frown. "For our sex, seeing a woman desirous of our member does much to inflate our pride."

"What is it you wish me to do?" she asked, a touch nervous.

He gestured to the floor before him. "Come here."

She climbed off the bed.

"On your knees."

Thus situated, her mouth was at the perfect height. He stroked himself as he took a step toward her. His member was stiff and inches from her face. She kept her eyes demurely downcast.

"Look at it. Is it not a beautiful instrument?" he asked.

"Yes, sir."

"Admire it."

She fixed her gaze, slightly cross eyed, at the pole pointed at her.

"With words," he clarified.

"It is a beautiful instrument."

"Did you enjoy having it inside of you?"

When she hesitated and looked away, he jolted her to attention by tugging her chin up.

"Yes, sir."

"Tell me you enjoyed having me inside you."

"I enjoyed having you inside me."

"Did you spend upon my member?"

"I did."

"Why?"

She returned a puzzled look.

"Why did you enjoy having me inside you? Why did you spend?"

After a moment of thought, she answered, "Because I am a wanton?"

"Well said. Your intelligence pleases me. Since you enjoy a man's member, I shall grant you more of it. You will take me into your mouth."

She balked. "Again?"

"You will learn to take it properly. Your husband will thank me for it. Do you not wish to please your husband?"

"I do, but…what you ask…"

"Is what? Wrong? Wanton? Devilish? It is all that, but trust me, your husband will have a newfound appreciation for you if you acquire this skill."

She did not appear convinced.

"The swallowing of a man's member is one of the greatest gifts you can give your husband in the bedchamber."

A drop of seed had leaked from the tip of his erection. He rubbed it over the head.

"Now open your mouth."

Still dubious, she stared at his shaft. He pinched her

nose shut, forcing her to take in air through her mouth. When her lips parted, he shoved himself between them. She started gagging immediately.

He gripped the back of her head. "It would have gone more smoothly had you obeyed me with promptness."

While holding her head in place, he gave her a reprieve and withdrew himself from her mouth. "Now if you wish me to go slowly and gently, you will do a better job of obeying. Do you understand?"

"Yes… sir."

"Now let us try that again. Open your mouth."

She opened her mouth, and he placed the crown of his cock inside her orifice.

"Now close your lips, not your teeth, about the tip."

He had to close his eyes and take a deep breath when her moist heat encased him. He had not fully expected she would comply but was thrilled with her present acquiescence, even if she did not know that it was her own husband's cock she took.

"Now a little more," he said, pushing another inch into her. "You will find it easier if you stay relaxed."

He slid the second inch into her. The rubbing of his cock upon her tongue was heavenly. But she started to gag. He pulled out of her and waited for her to collect herself.

"I cannot do it," she protested.

"You can and you will. If you have the patience to learn how to play the Concerto in C Major by Mozart, you have the ability to learn to swallow a man's member. Let us try again."

She parted her lips. He replaced his cock and attempted three inches this time. She gagged once more.

"Relax," he reminded her.

But their next attempt led to more gagging and coughing.

"Stand up," he decided.

With relief, she scrambled to her feet. He reached a hand between her thighs and caressed the moist flesh there. She gave a soft moan. He fondled her clitoris, slick with the nectar of her arousal, till she panted and whimpered. He slid a digit into her quim. She was a furnace of desire.

"My God," he breathed. "Do you know how hot and wet you are?"

"No, sir," she replied weakly.

When he curled his finger and stroked, she gasped. He fit a second digit in while his thumb took over the ministrations upon her clitoris. Her body began to tremble.

"It would seem you wish to spend again, my slut," he noted after several minutes. "Do you?"

"Yes, sir."

"Then you must earn the privilege."

He pushed her back down onto her knees and pointed his cock at her mouth. "Open."

Like a hatchling waiting for nourishment, she opened her mouth. He placed himself inside her. She stifled her gag and closed her lips about his shaft. She had but half his length, but it felt wondrous. He fisted his hand into her hair and pushed more of himself in. He could see her fighting the urge to choke.

"Relax," he urged in a soothing tone, "and keep your mouth closed. Yes, like that. Good."

Slowly, he withdrew, relishing the tug of her lips upon his girth. As gently as he could, he eased himself back in. For a moment, he savored the sensation of being cradled upon her tongue before repeating the motion, making sure he did not push too far. When she became more accustomed to having him in her mouth, he attempted more. His cods were boiling, and he had to clench the muscles of his arse to keep from shoving into her. Pulling out, he saw his shaft glisten with her saliva.

He replaced his erection in her mouth. When she wrapped her lips about him and sucked, shivers went down his legs. He did his best to take her mouth gently, but she felt too delightful. His ardor had waited long enough. He began thrusting more vigorously, more deeply. She gagged when his tip hit the back of her throat. He tried his best to more gently, though it was no easy feat when he was but a hair's length from rapture.

He erupted. With a roar, he bucked his hips. Unable to keep pace, she pushed herself away. He released her and stumbled back, quakes ravaging his body. As this was her first time taking cock, she could not best his mistress, but the fact that it was Trudie and the wicked satisfaction he received from compelling his unfaithful wife into an act of such wantonness was surprisingly titillating.

Letting out a haggard breath, he knelt before her. With his seed glistening upon her lips and chin, she was a lovely sight. He kissed the top of her brow. "Well done, my dear. You have a fortunate husband."

She surprised him with a small smile. He returned it with his own. He was not finished with her. She had shown great promise, and there was much he had in store for her. Hers was going to be a long night, but one that would be worth her while.

Chapter Nine

NEVER BEFORE COULD TRUDIE have imagined finding herself in such degradation. She half knelt, half lay with her face down upon the bed and her derrière propped in the air. Her ankles were spread and tied to opposing bedposts, and her arms were pinned beneath her body. A stocking of hers had been used to tie her wrists between her knees. In this position, with not a shred of clothing upon her, she was exposed in a most lewd and wanton fashion. As if to call attention to this, he blew upon her *there*. She felt his warm breath between her buttocks, upon the intimate folds and hairs just below her rump.

She shut her eyes, as if doing so could transport her to a different actuality. Had she truly agreed to this? Half of her wished her friend, Diana, would return and rescue her from this lewd position. The other half would be mortified for anyone to find her so displayed.

A warm and firm hand palmed her buttock. Her body nearly catapulted off the bed. Till tonight, no one had ever purposefully lain a hand upon her backside. Not even Leopold.

"Such a lovely arse," he murmured. "There is much more we can do with its potential."

Her face flushed to recall the spanking she had received at his hand. It was folly. Every bit of it. And yet, she found herself acquiescing.

Gently, he caressed the curve of a cheek before giving it a light slap. Her mind raced at what she ought to expect next from him. At times he had seemed vexed with her, and this unsettled her for she knew not why. He had seduced her with seeming deliberation. But perhaps he had hoped to find a better partner for his time here at Château Follet and was disgruntled that she was all that remained.

"Dear God," she cried, shuddering, for he had touched the flesh between her thighs.

"The sensitivity of your body is unparalleled," he remarked.

Her breath caught, and she could not speak, not even to plead that he be gentle with her.

She felt the bed lift with the removal of his weight. With the side of her head pressed into the bed, she could not see the part of the room he roamed.

Dread filled her as a giggle escaped her lips. Softness, perhaps that of a feather, brushed the bottom of her right foot.

"I had forgotten how ticklish you can be," he murmured to himself.

She found the statement odd for they had not been in each other's company for long, but she did not dwell upon for it for she was far too anxious at what he might do.

"This should prove amusing sport," he said before

grazing the plume against the bottom of her other foot.

She could not suppress the giggling and squirmed against her bonds. There was a reprieve. She curled her toes.

"The arch of the foot is among the most sensitive of body parts," he explained and demonstrated with more tickling.

"Oh! G—!"

Her words were swallowed by her own laughs. She could not contain herself. It was not possible to brace her feet against the onslaught. She wriggled and strained to get away. Just when she thought she could take no more, he withdrew. She took in several ragged breaths.

"Did you know a mere ostrich plume could prove so lethal a weapon?" he asked.

When she did not respond, he brushed the plume along a buttock. Though it was not as awful as the bottoms of her feet, she cried out.

"Yes! No!" she replied. "No, I did not."

"I thank your bonnet for providing the implement, but worry not, I shall return the plume to the headdress when we are finished."

She would have preferred that he did not. She needed no reminders of her time here and certainly no reminders of how he had used the plume upon her. He brushed the feather next over the curve of her back, making her gasp for breath. When he returned to stroking the plume across the arch of her foot, tears pressed against her eyes.

"Pl—Please!" she cried. "Enough!"

Pausing, he allowed her space to draw in much needed air. "Do you require your safety word?"

Her breath haggard, she considered the option.

"Perhaps we should stop altogether," he said. "I had not intended a feather to prove such a punishment more exquisite lessons."

Not wanting to appear ridiculous if tickling should prove too much abuse for her to take, she replied, "No. Please continue."

The plume moved up her inner thigh, and she bore this better than upon the soles of her feet. Slowly, the plume neared her quim, teasingly close. She whimpered, remembering how it had felt to be pleasured by him there. She was mindful once more of how exposed she felt, her most intimate parts accessible by view and touch.

As if reading her thoughts, he followed the plume with his hand, grazing her thigh lightly. She quivered. Would he touch her intimately? As he had done in the piano room and several times after? She hoped not. Or did she?

His hand was warm and gentle upon her, but she was still unaccustomed to his caresses. Moreover, it was wrong. Despite having the word of safety, her bonds made her feel helpless. What if he chose not to honor the word of safety? He could do to her whatever he wished. It was foolish of her to have exposed herself thusly. He might discover her true identity.

She groaned when he moved his hand to the top of her thigh and over to her folds. He found that nub of pleasure without a second to spare. What did he intend? For a moment she wished he would return to tickling her instead. Her breath hitched as he toyed with that bud, stoking those agonizing ripples in her loins. How was it her body should be so responsive to his touch? Her body would betray her even if every ounce of forbearance cautioned against that sweet torture. His caresses were simply too exquisite. Despite herself, she found herself craving more, as if she had not already found satiation and spent. Or perhaps it was because she had. Was it possible that spending primed her body to want more? Like a single bite of confection was not enough.

His languid and attentive strokes had her panting and grunting. What a weakling she was! How could she be so devoid of character of a sudden? Lust soon overcame her disappointment as his fondling brought her higher toward rapture. This time she did not fear the strange yet enthralling agitation building inside her. She knew it was well worth the ecstasy that awaited on the other side of the precipice.

But to her surprise, he withdrew his hand. He wiped her wetness on a buttock. The area between her thighs ached and throbbed in his absence. The discomfort of being bereft permeated her to her core. In that moment, she preferred the tickling.

"You know that I could do anything to you right now?"

"Yes."

"And how do you feel about that—do you think

your husband would like to see you thus?" She swallowed. "And you, would you like him to pleasure you, and himself, in this way?"

Now would be an opening to reconsider this path she had ventured down, but no words came to her.

He called her attention by swatting a buttock.

She gasped. "Y-yes."

He rewarded her by touching her between the legs, his caresses easily reawakening her arousal. She gave herself into the beautiful sensations welling in her lower body.

"Ah, my dear, not yet. You may not spend until I say. Delay immediate gratification and you shall find the pleasure you seek more exquisite."

She panted and moaned lightly. Her body teetered on the precipice, but she nodded and focused on him. He returned to fondling her quim. Her climactic euphoria could wash away all other sensations, all thoughts.

"Your husband must want to see you thus, in the throes of pleasure, vital and waiting."

"Please, I..."

His ministrations, his teasing of her flesh, brought her to again to the precipice and tumbled her over into the sea of ecstasy. Her body erupted in shivers. For several seconds, she knew nothing but pleasure.

After wringing the last of the tremors from her body, he remained still and quiet while she basked in the glow of carnal satiation.

"Thank you, sir."

* * * * *

Standing behind her, he returned to stroking her flesh. She groaned, in relief, in desire, in frustration that she could not utter the words that would end this. His fingers caused a new heat to burn. She pressed herself into his hand, desperate for the release that would diminish the aching in her chest. He sank two digits into the seat of her wetness and touched a part of her that sent her reeling. The discomfort of her position began to fade in favor of the delicious sensations lancing through her. Her cries now were of a different nature. He coaxed her toward the plateau she sought with surprising swiftness. Her body gloried in his abilities, though a small part of her wished she had never known his touch for she worried that nothing else could ever match its potency and beauty. With a devastating cry, she fell into paroxysm, her body jerking and bucking against his hand and into the bed. This was the most delightful of experiences. It was certain her body would know no finer pleasure.

She lay, relishing the sweet hum in her body. The blood still pulsed between her legs, down her legs, and even in her toes. She had asked for lessons, but he had gifted her pleasure along with them. But, when she felt him rubbing her foot, she knew he was not yet done. His thumb caressed the arch of her foot. He employed the plume again. Her body, already in a heightened state of pure sensation, could not stand even this light touch.

She laughed in agony and jerked against her bonds, but he held her foot fast. He tickled her till fresh tears brimmed in her eyes. She would have preferred in that instant to have been a paraplegic. Just as she thought she could not catch her breath amidst her laughs, he stopped.

"You have a delightful laugh."

Her face pressed into the bed. She could barely move enough to speak, even if she could. He seemed to sense her thoughts and untied her hands. Rubbing her wrists gently, he then retied them to the bed posts, so that her arms stretched on either side. He assisted her to move her legs up as well, so she could lift her head more easily.

"Is that better?"

"Yes. Thank you," she answered.

"You are to be commended, my dear. Indeed, you are doing as well as many a veteran of Château Follett."

"Thank you, sir."

"I shall repeat: You have a delightful laugh."

"Thank you."

"Good. A gentleman likes his compliments acknowledged. Do you like compliments? I believe you are that rare woman who does not."

"Yes, I mean, no." She let her body relax into the bed again, her head a muddle from the storm brewing in her body.

The bed sank for he had climbed atop it. She felt his fingers strum her bud of pleasure. Through the aching of head and the trembling of her body, beautiful sensations managed to blossom between her legs. She was all confusion. A part of her wanted to curl in a corner and sob till her tears emptied. Another wanted only to exalt in the pleasure he was able to command. She moaned as the tension in her womanhood began to build.

She heard the rustle of clothing, then felt his velvet hardness at her folds. His rod slid along her wetness. Her sensations heightened in both alarm and desire. She yearned for and feared his penetration. As he drew his length between her nether lips, she tilted toward the former. Her mind desperately cautioned her against wanting this. It was wrong. She would undo all the penance she had suffered by breaching her marital vows again. To want this was madness.

But her body had partaken of the poisoned apple and craved the forbidden fruit. The temptation between her legs was too great. She wanted that euphoric rush, wanted it to wipe away her doubts and fears.

"Do you wish to spend again?"

"Yes," she moaned.

"Do you wish me to ravish you?"

She groaned. She did not want to risk it, but his stroking had ignited a fire that needed to be doused.

"Yes."

"You deserve to be ravished well, my dear."

That said, he sank himself into her. She groaned at the unfamiliar stretching inside her. A slight rawness remained from being taken earlier, but the discomfort soon faded, replaced by a most delicious tension. She wanted him to fuel the aggravation in her loins. He obliged with a slow and steady thrusting.

She sniffed then groaned. "Oh…"

"Does it please you, my dear?"

Most assuredly. Aloud, she said, "Yes."

"You enjoy being fucked."

With each thrust of his, she felt the heavens descend closer toward her. Nothing mattered but the euphoria awaiting her.

"Do you enjoy being taken by a man not your husband?"

This jolted her, interrupting her journey through carnal paradise.

"Answer me. Do you enjoy being taken by a man not your husband?"

"N-No."

He pulled out. She gasped at the emptiness. Her body rioted at the withdrawal.

"Are you quite certain of that?" he asked as his tip toyed with her opening.

"No… I am not certain."

"Then you do wish me to take you?"

She whimpered. "Yes. Please… Take me."

"And ravish you?"

"Please ravish me," she whispered.

She tried to feel his shaft grazing her between her thighs.

"You wish me to ravish you."

Had that not already been established? she wanted to retort, but she wallowed too much in misery to accomplish a rejoinder. Perhaps there was still hope that she had enough forbearance to overcome her venereal cravings.

But when he plunged himself back inside her, she was lost. He varied the rhythm and intensity of his thrusting.

"Is this how you wish to be ravished?"

"Yes," she uttered between grunting and groaning. Her climax emerged upon the horizon.

He held onto her hips, his motions purposeful as he stroked the lovely frenzy.

"Tell me, have he always enjoyed being taken in such lewd fashion?"

His words burned her ears, but she had to admit, as degrading as the position was, it felt marvelous. His penetration deepened, his pelvis slapping into her derrière.

"Answer me."

"Yes."

"And why is it you enjoy this manner?"

She braced herself against the tide of pleasure, a part of her still afraid of the force of sensations threatening to overwhelm her body.

"Because I am a wanton harlot." She knew not where the words had come from, and he, too, seemed surprised for he paused.

"Well, well. That you are. And it is my pleasure to oblige a harlot such as yourself."

He resumed bucking against her. She cried out she began to ascend the waves.

"You are quite the delightful harlot. One that needs and desires to be ravished all night long."

She peaked. He drilled deeper and harder as ecstasy crashed into her, drowning her in divine paroxysm. She was not conscious of his tightening grip upon her hips or the increased force of his pounding. She felt herself soaring to heights she had never before known. The intensity of it was otherworldly.

He slammed himself into her. He roared and pulled from her. Liquid heat rained on her legs. A small voice cautioned that she played a dangerous gamble. But that did not matter in the moment. She had been catapulted into the heavens, and she knew not that she would return.

Chapter Ten

TRUDIE LAY UPON HER side, still in a daze. Moments ago, she had been floating, her body brought to heights she had never before known existed.

The bonds had been removed from her wrists and ankles. Though she was free to move, she remained where she was upon the bed, drawing in a deep breath as she tried to put together a coherent thought. The throbbing between her thighs and the pulsing in her limbs had faded. After the euphoria had ebbed, a hollowness emerged.

He had ravished her. At her own behest. Though she had found more pleasure than she had ever thought possible, what price had it come at?

She sat up, pulled away from him and sat up. She had agreed to suffer penance for her crimes, in the hopes that her guilt would be lessened. But he had made her spend, had taken her once more, and made her guilty of adultery anew. She felt the viscous evidence of her infidelity between her legs. Anger and shame quaked inside her.

"You will want refreshment after what you have endured," he said, standing before her. "I will procure for you drink and sustenance. After you have partaken of some refreshments, we shall continue with your lesson."

He kissed her on the brow before departing. It was an odd gesture and seemed almost affectionate, but Trudie would grant him no allowances. She failed to understand how her body could respond so favorably to him but that the carnal must be wholly separate from the mind.

And he expected to *continue* with her lesson! She could suffer no more at the man's hands.

After he had departed, she rose from the bed. She would dress but feared doing so would delay her escape. Grabbing a robe, she slid into it and hurried out the door.

Out in the corridor, she knew not where to head but determined she would put as much distance between herself and her debaucher as possible. In bare feet, she scurried through the hall and was cognizant that she had entered a different part of the Château for the flooring and walls had changed. She slowed when she heard voices, one familiar to her ears.

Diana. Her husband's cousin.

"No need to tarry out here, mademoiselle," said a man who had come up behind her. "You'll have a much better view inside."

Grabbing her hand, he pulled her into the room. Luckily for Trudie, he released her when a woman pounced upon him and drew all his attentions.

Nearly a dozen men and women, in various states

of dress, occupied the room filled with sofas and tables set about a mound of pillows in the middle of the room.

"Trudie!" Diana waved her over.

Without her mask, Trudie did not feel comfortable in extended company, but she had no wish to encounter her debaucher. Feeling safer with Diana, she went to take a seat beside her friend upon a divan.

"Where is your night's paramour?" Diana asked.

"He and I are done," Trudie replied and hoped that her friend would not ask for particulars.

"Then you are free to enjoy in the revelry here!" Diana handed her a glass of wine. "Madame Follet has a fine cellar. You'll not find a better claret."

Trudie took the glass. Though she did not partake of wine often, she finished the glass rather promptly.

Diana raised her brows and motioned for one of the footmen, scantily clad in nothing but a Roman toga, to approach. "Another glass for my friend."

Trudie opened her mouth to object but Diana spoke over her. "Does Château Follet not exceed expectations? La! I wonder that I had waited as long as I had before coming? How silly I was to have thought my husband would give up his mistress! But at last I have found a proper divertissement for me, and I vow it were much more exciting than what Charles must have with his lightskirt! You saw the Adonis I found. Is he not far more handsome than Charles?"

Trudie would have looked for the man Diana had paired with for the evening but found it too unsettling to observe some of the guests, a few of whom were in engaged in amorous activity. Her cheeks reddened at glimpsing a couple brazenly petting one another, and she promptly decided that staring into her empty glass was a safer way to past the time.

"He has gone in search of the perfect Champenois wine," Diana supplied. "I told him I adored the sparkle and the bubbles."

Trudie watched Diana recline at an angle and wished she had her friend's ease. One would have thought Diana to be a frequent guest of the Château. Trudie, in contrast, still harbored the desire to flee. But as the hour was very late, she could not. And courtesy would not allow her to depart without her friend. Thus, she was trapped.

A part of her wanted to reveal the details of what had transpired to Diana, to seek her counsel and her solace. As she observed the merriment in Diana's countenance, however, she decided to keep her own woes to herself rather than dampen her friend's mood.

But Diana noticed her less than cheerful disposition.

"Why so glum?" Diana asked. "Do you miss your lover? Did he desert you?"

Trudie shook her head.

Diana leaned in. "Was he all that you had hoped for in a lover?"

"Goodness, no!" Trudie replied. "I mean…he was…"

"I can tell by the blush in your cheeks that he must have been, at the least, decent."

Blushing further, Trudie did not know how to respond. Her debaucher had made her spend despite the mental agony of her situation.

"Perhaps our lovers would consider swapping?" Diana mused aloud. "I am curious to know what your lover is like. Mine has been more than satisfactory, I assure you."

Trudie's mind whirled. She had sinned with one man and could not contemplate committing adultery with a second.

"We have an entertaining enactment," Diana purred. "I am his 'lovely little slave,' as he calls me, and he is my 'Master Aries.' I must do his every bidding, and I serve him gladly for the rewards are *delicious*."

"If you do not perform his bidding, what happens then?"

"I always do as he wishes."

"There are no consequences?"

"I should hope not...or perhaps it would be rather fun to see what he would do...We are merely playing roles. Ah, my master approaches with the wine!"

Diana's Adonis of flaxen hair approached with a bottle in hand.

"And who is your friend?" he asked of Diana as he sat beside her.

"This is my cousin-in-law," Diana replied, holding up her glass for him to fill.

"Is she joining us for a *menage-a-trois*?"

Heat flared in Trudie's cheeks.

"She is spoken for," Diana answered for Trudie.

"Thus, you must make any arrangements with her lover first."

"And where is he?"

"I know not," Trudie answered quickly, rather terrified that the man would seek out her debaucher.

"How is you do not know? He left you to fend for yourself on your first evening?"

"He...had other matters to attend."

"Darling," Diana interjected, "this wine is delightful. You must try it!"

Master Aries poured a glass for Trudie.

"I could drink this all day!" Diana said and held up her empty glass once more.

As he filled it, Trudie took a sip of hers. It was a cheerful wine and only mildly bitter.

"Do you not like it?" Diana inquired after swallowing it as easily as if it were milk tea.

"Careful," Master Aries said. "The effervescence makes inebriation faster than you would suspect. Perhaps I should hold your glass."

Diana giggled as he held her glass for her to sip from. Feeling a little awkward witnessing them, Trudie continued to drink her wine. She turned her gaze to a couple lying amid a bed of pillows in the center of the room.

The man and the woman were both naked. Trudie wondered that they had the courage to display themselves in such audacious and wanton fashion. They must be quite intoxicated. The woman lay stretched before her partner, her black tresses spread out among the pillows, a contrast to her alabaster skin. The woman groped her own breasts, rolling them over her chest as the man looked on, stroking his member. She spread her legs wide, a clear invitation. They would engage in congress in public, Trudie realized. With his free hand, the man caressed her crotch. She moaned and tugged at her nipples. For several minutes, they continued in this manner. He stroked himself, then her, then himself again. She began to writhe with her moans.

Trudie took another sip of her wine, only to find the glass empty. How had she finished it so quickly?

"Do you wish for more?" asked Master Aries.

"Perhaps a little more," replied Trudie.

He refilled her glass for her. Trudie returned to looking at the naked couple in the middle of the room. There was something utterly inappropriate and completely naughty in watching the private corporal acts of another, yet curiosity won over guilt and shame. After all, she was not watching them in secret. Nay, the couple flaunted what they did. The man began to slide his member along the woman's folds.

With a grunt, the man sank into his companion. Trudie's mouth dropped.

"Mmm, I should like to be her," Diana murmured.

From the corners of her eyes, Trudie saw Diana's hand pull at her own skirts.

"Allow me," Master Aries said.

Flushing, Trudie fixed her attention upon her wine and the couple in the center of the room. Every time the man bucked his hips, the woman groaned with evident pleasure. Trudie wondered that the woman could feel not the slightest discomfort being exposed to all, roughly taken by this man on the floor of the room.

Beside her, Trudie could hear Diana faintly panting.

The woman cried out in evident pleasure. The man followed not long after, roaring as if he had injured himself something fierce.

Trudie realized she felt exceptionally warm and that an agitation swirled gently below her navel. She found she rather envied the woman laying prone upon the pillows.

Diana gave a great sigh and mumbled, "That was rather delightful."

"Another glass, my dear?" asked Master Aries. "I see your friend may need another as well."

Trudie looked down at her empty glass.

"Shall I bring another bottle?" asked a footman.

"If you will show me to Madame's cellar, I should like to select my own."

"I wish to go as well," Diana said, leaping to her feet. "You were gone far too long last time. Come, Trudie, lest you prefer to remain here?"

Trudie rose to her feet. She did not wish to be in a roomful of strangers, and a walk about might clear her head. Then she would decide what to do with the remainder of the night.

Chapter Eleven

A FAINT BUT UNCOMFORTABLE throbbing persisted like a vise about her head. Trudie fluttered her eyelids, glad for the dimness of her surroundings. She had fallen asleep, and part of her wanted to remain in slumber, but all was not right.

She could not remember where she had fallen asleep. Memories of a woman being taken by a naked man in a room full of strangers danced in and out of her consciousness. She recalled the thrusting of the man, how the woman palmed her own breasts and grunted with pleasure being filled by him. Trudie remembered attempting to douse with champagne the rising lust in her own body. She had consumed too much. That was why she had fallen asleep. But she did not recall drifting off to sleep in the salon. She had been with Diana and Diana's paramour. And there was another. One of the footmen. She did not remember his name. She had been in their company. Diana and her paramour had stumbled off somewhere, leaving Trudie alone with the footman. That was the last of what she remembered before falling asleep.

Realizing her discomfort extended to other parts of

her body, Trudie attempted to adjust herself, but she could not move. Opening her eyes wide, she saw that she was not in the salon, nor the cellar where Madame Follett kept her wine, but a new chamber altogether. And the reason she could not move was because she was bound to the bed again, as she had been earlier, her wrists tied to the posts. Her head felt heavy, her confusion and upset greater than it had been before. Had the footman tied her in this manner? Her body felt as if it had been tossed about in a post chaise on a bad road. Even her jaw felt sore, with spittle drooling down the sides of her mouth because she must have fallen asleep with her mouth open. What humiliation was to be endured now? She tried not to panic. "Awake at last."

It was the voice of her debaucher. She could not decide if she was relieved or not.

She decided not.

Though she could not see him as he was somewhere in the shadows of the room, she could hear his footsteps. She heard the sound of liquid being poured into a glass.

Where had Diana gone off to? Trudie struggled against her bonds.

"I would not waste the energy were I you," he said. "You will require it to last the night."

He stepped into her view, and she saw that, unlike her, he was fully clothed save that he had foregone a coat. He cupped her chin and lifted her head. In the dim lighting of the room, she could not make out the expression in his eyes from behind his mask, but from the firm set of his jaw, she believed she had much to fear. She did not believe she could endure any more, not even pleasure.

"I had not given you permission to leave," he continued, "thus, I was quite disappointed to find you gone when I returned. You realize you will have to learn from your lack of regard."

She gave a despairing moan as he released her chin and let her head fall.

"But I think you will be up for the task for you are much more the wanton creature than I thought. Perhaps I had not made clear the arrangements betwixt you and I. While we are here, and together, you are mine and mine alone. I had procured some ratafia among your refreshments, but given your inebriation, I think water best."

He lifted her head again and bade her drink. "It is naught but water," he said, taking a sip to demonstrate it was not poisonous.

He presented the water to her once more, and this time she drank it readily, hoping it would dilute the thickness in her head.

"I'm sorry," she mumbled after she had finished.

"Sorry that you were caught?"

Well, of course that. But she did not speak anything that might perturb him.

"I am disappointed that you found it necessary to abscond my company. Though you are a novice, your wantonness and willingness impressed me till now. But you have apparently found me lacking."

She furrowed her brow, perplexed.

"My company was insufficient for you as you chose to seek that of another."

"You frightened me," she confessed.

"And you did not find the footman intimidating."

"The footman?"

"Yes, I found the two of you in the cellar, your legs spread wider than a slut's beneath him."

Her eyes widened. "I did not..." Her mind strained to recall what could have transpired.

"When I discovered you missing," he said, "I went looking for you. By chance, I came across your friend, Diana. She told me you were in the wine cellar with a friend."

"I can't remember," Trudie protested. "I would have—I don't even know the man!"

"Then it is all the more naughty and wanton of you."

Dear God, had she committed adultery with a second man in one night? She remembered the champagne. Regret, its brutal blades twisting inside of her, made her want to curl in a corner and disappear. How could she have done such a thing? She should not have allowed herself to consume so much wine. Coming to Château Follet was the most grievous error of her life.

"I suppose you could affix the blame upon your intoxication, but can you truthfully say that you would not have lifted your skirts beneath the footman were you sober?"

Trudie was at a loss for words because she felt as if she no longer knew herself. Her silence seemed to displease him for his lips formed a grim line. "I promise you, after we are done, you will not want to desert me again."

* * * * *

Trudie groaned. This did not bode well. He caressed then squeezed her breasts, tweaking each nipple between thumb and forefinger. She was fully awake now.

"Such lovely breasts merit attention," he said.

She took in long, loud breaths through her nose as she watched him go to the sideboard and retrieve a bottle. Ambling to her, he set the bottle on the nightstand. He uncapped it and poured out what appeared to be oil upon his hands. "With this, you shall need to remain naked for some time, lest you wish to soil your garments." He smiled, as if he wanted her to be always naked. "My God, you have lovely teats. We must anoint them."

He rubbed his hands together over her, droplets of oil flecking her bare skin. With feather-light strokes, he eased his hands on her chest, first under her breasts, then on the sensitive flesh and nipples. The warmth, nay tenderness, of his touch caused such a war of sadness and tenderness that she could not move. Then his hand wandered between her thighs, prying apart the folds to reach that nub of betrayal. She strained and jerked

113

against the ropes. He would undo her once more. He slapped a breast to still her and she did her best to settle her body, but it was no easy feat for that little nub of flesh held such potency. Even the gentlest stroke of his finger was agonizing. She did not understand how it could be so when apprehension still gripped her.

"I want you to spend for me."

She shook her head. How could she knowing what she did, and he did not? "No."

To her dismay, he dotted more oil on his fingers and worked at her nub. The oil slicked and warmed in such a way that she could not bear it, yet she arched into his touch. These sensations so echoed those in her mind and heart that all she craved was release, and he could give that to her, if she would let him. He stopped his touches. "You will spend for me now, I think."

She nodded, relief washing over her when he again resumed his attentions. He caressed her between the legs. "And do not presume to fool me," he said. "I know enough of your body to discern whether it has truly spent. You have no wish to deceive me."

His thumb pressed upon that most sensitive rosebud. Pleasure flared. To her surprise, his continued fondling had caused her to grow wetter than ever. What did this mean? Why was this so? As he strummed her traitorous bud, he teased the opening of her slit. She was still a little sore from his earlier penetration but found herself wanting him to enter. She shivered when his digit passed over the opening and moaned when he sank a tip inside. His entry both satisfied and stoked the lust burning within her.

"Allow the pleasure to prevail," he coaxed.

She shook her head. She deserved no pleasure, ought derive no pleasure from what he did to her. Spending would give him the false indication that she wanted this treatment. But concentrated shudders went through her when he curled two fingers inside her.

Good heavens! How was he able to draw such intensity, his fingers eliciting reverberations as if her body was a tuning fork he had struck?

"I think you will spend, whether you desire it or no," he commented.

He spoke true. She could not fight against the tide, her body now jerking of its own accord. The wave would slam into her, and there was nothing she could do to prevent it from crushing her, till she became naught but a bundle of vibrating nerves, thousands upon thousands of nerves.

His fingers stroked and stroked, past her wails of dismay as her body triumphed, still buried inside her even as she writhed and flailed, unable to contain the burst of pleasure.

"My God," he breathed.

How she had managed to remain in one piece, one body, she knew not. She quietly sobbed, partially in glee, grateful for the unprecedented euphoria, and partially in sorrow, for having lost her battle.

But it was a most sublime loss.

Chapter Twelve

LEOPOLD BEHELD HIS WIFE. The blush of arousal colored her rounded cheeks, and her thick lashes fluttered as the last wave of ecstasy moved through her. Naked, her hair in disarray, she had never looked more beautiful to him. He slid his fingers from the warm, wet clutch of her quim. Her head lolled, as it had when he had carried her unconscious body from the wine cellar to this room.

Anger pulsed in his groin as he recalled the scene he had stumbled upon over an hour ago. He had brought a tray of lemonade, sweetmeats, and biscuits to Trudie's chamber, excited for all that he intended to show her, proud that his timid wife had blossomed into such a wanton, only to find the room empty. She had left without permission.

At first, he had felt remorseful. Perhaps he had been too harsh with her. She would have to pay the price of disobedience, but his ire had not been raised until he saw her, his cousin Diana, and two other men heading to the stairs that led to the kitchen and cellar. From her unsteady gait, he could see Trudie was in the cups. He had never witnessed his wife inebriated. He suspected it was because of Diana, who had laughed and giggled loudly, as she clung to the arm of her paramour. Leopold had reminded himself to speak with Charles, her husband, to keep a tighter leash upon Diana. He would not normally have cared so much except for her influence upon Trudie.

Leopold had waited for the foursome to return, but only Diana and her paramour, holding a bottle of champagne, emerged. After waiting a few minutes more and still Trudie did not show, Leopold had hurried downstairs to find her in a daze, her legs spread wide, in the corner of the cellar beside the racks of wine. A young man—one of the footmen—knelt before her, holding his erection. He had scrambled to his feet when Leopold had barked at him.

Grasping him by the front of his linen, Leopold had threatened to kick him out of the Château, before tossing the servant away. Leopold had felt the veins in his neck throb. He was cross with the footman for pressing his advantage with an inebriated woman and at the foolishness of his wife. How could she have allowed herself to become so intoxicated? He would not have thought Trudie to possess a reckless bone in her body. Here at Château Follet, however, her qualities surprised him. But, for certain, she would never have come to the Château if not for Diana. Leopold had had a mind to deliver the lesson Diana merited. He doubted Charles capable of doing so properly.

Leopold eyed the chamber he had brought Trudie to. Trudie was completely new to Château Follet. Her unease and discomfort when he had first seduced her this night had been obvious.

But she needed to be taught a lesson. To his surprise, she had wanted it. Wanted the corporal sensations to drown her feelings of guilt. Though she had only had congress with her husband here at Château Follet, in her mind, she had lain with a man other than her husband. In her mind, the adultery was true. At times, he had thought she might recognize him from behind his mask. A few times, he had forgotten to disguise his voice. But she had been too lost in her debauchery to notice. And now, she had spread her legs before one who was most definitely not her husband. A servant. Her wrongs tonight were now many. She did not deserve the pleasure he had granted her body till now, but he needed to ascertain that the fear he had seen in her eyes would not overwhelm all that he did or all that he was yet to do, and the rapture would help sustain the education that awaited her.

He took in the scent of her arousal upon his fingers, then slid them over her plump lips that she could taste herself upon him. She furrowed her brow.

"Where are your manners?" he asked.

Seeing the confusion in her countenance, he tugged on a nipple. She gave a cry before mumbling, "Thank you."

"Much better."

She whimpered as he rolled the aching little buds between his thumbs and forefingers, making her breasts protrude. Her areolas were the largest he had ever seen. His arousal stretched as he gazed upon her beautiful bosom.

"I was most sorry to find you gone when I returned," he said, noting that she did not meet his gaze. "My pride was further wounded when I discovered you with the footman. I had no notion you are such a gluttonous little whore. One cock is not sufficient for you, but it is my aim to give you more than enough."

She had looked up at him in alarm when he had mentioned the footman. Perhaps she did not remember. It mattered not. He began to unbutton his fall.

"Tell me, how did you enjoy congress with the footman?"

"I did not," she protested

"You did not taste him before you invited him between your legs?"

Her lips, sweet and plump, formed a frown. "I could not have—I would not have…"

He stroked the member he had freed from his breeches. Her breath grew uneven immediately upon seeing it.

"What would your husband think if he knew you had been given a gown of green by a common servant?"

She shook her head. "I was—I had consumed too much wine. I did not anticipate the effects of it. I would not have willingly submitted myself."

"No? You were wet for him."

He saw her mind reeling.

"There was no denying the evidence of your wantonness. I discovered much of it dripping down your thighs."

She flushed crimson. "That must've been because…"

"Because of what?"

She swallowed. "Because of what I saw earlier."

"What did you see?" he inquired, intrigued.

She lowered her gaze. "I witnessed a woman being pleasured."

"Indeed? How so?"

"By a man."

"And how did he please her?"

She hesitated until he tweaked a nipple. "He was settled between her legs."

"And you found the scene delightful?"

When she did not answer, he pinched her other nipple.

"I did."

"Did this woman enjoy being taken before others?"

"She appeared to."

"Do you?"

"Please…"

"A lascivious harlot such as yourself must have enjoyed bearing witness." He pointed his erection at her lips. "Come. Demonstrate your prurience."

"But I—"

She stopped when he reached for her nipple. She opened her mouth. As with the first time, she gagged at the unnatural intrusion, but he held her head in place, forcing her to find a way to adjust. She wrapped her lips over his rod, and he closed his eyes to relish the beautiful warmth embracing him.

"You are a quick student and have improved much in so short a time," he commented when he began to saw his rod in and out of her orifice and felt less of her teeth against him. Pulling back, he aimed his cock at an angle to see the tip pushing out her cheek. "Your husband will be much pleased. I think he would not have expected his wife to swallow perform so well."

He pulled out of her mouth and wiped the moisture across her lips. "You must promise to take your husband's shaft often so that your instruction here will not go to waste."

When she did not answer, he wrapped her hair around his right hand and tugged her gaze to meet his. "Promise."

She stared, distraught. A tear seemed to glisten in the corner of one eye. He did his best to ignore it, reminding himself that she had brought this upon herself.

"Promise," he repeated.

"Please..."

"He will not know to ask it of you. Thus, you must offer yourself to him. Does he not deserve some manner of benefit from your adultery?"

Her distress disappeared for the moment, replaced by anguish. "What benefit have I derived from his?"

He stifled his guilt and replied, "It is common for husbands to take mistresses."

"And for that his wrong is less than mine?"

"No," he said after a moment's consideration, "but was your motive in coming here to right a wrong or to match his infidelity with your own?"

She looked away and said in a despairing moan, "And for what purpose do you concern yourself? Is it to debase me?"

"Did you not wish for lessons in both penance and pleasure?"

"I will forever rue the day I came here," she whispered. "My soul is eternally damned."

"Did we not establish that your lessons may serve several purposes."

"*Your* purposes?"

"If you could atone for making your husband a cuckold, would you?"

"Yes."

"You indicated an interest in pleasing your husband. Do you not wish to please him in the bedchamber?"

"He is satisfied by another," she muttered.

"You wanted to be more proficient than his mistress."

"It is not possible."

Hearing her dejection, he knelt down to meet her gaze. He rubbed his thumb over her lower lip. "I promised you that I could teach you all you need know. Your husband will want for no other."

The prospect obviously tempted her, but she murmured with doubt, "It is of no use. His mistress is far prettier—"

"Ah, but your husband has not seen how beautifully you spend. Its beauty would rival that of Helen of Troy."

Her breath stalled.

"I assure you your husband would be eternally grateful to me."

She shook her head. "You mock me, sir. It pleases you and serves you to have me your willing whore."

"What is to be gained if you were left to yourself now? So that you might nurse your wounds, your shame, and crawl back to your husband a lesser wife than you were before? Or do you wish to learn how to pleasure a man so that he desires you with every fiber of his being?"

"Whores can be had anywhere."

"Not your sort."

When she said nothing, he added, "I promise your husband will be pleased, and I do not make promises lightly."

He rose and pointed his erection once more at her mouth. She stared at his cock in silence, then opened her mouth. In triumph, he shoved himself in a little too harshly. She choked. He waited till her coughing settled and inserted himself more slowly this time.

"Lick the tip," he directed. "Now the crown. Suckle it."

He groaned in approval as her tongue circled the flare of his cock before she wrapped her warm, wet lips about him. He pushed himself in deeper.

"Harder."

Her cheeks caved inward in her efforts. A thrill shivered down his legs. He shoved himself deeper. A part of him still wanted to punish her with his member, but he forced himself to retreat. When she had collected herself, he slid himself in gently. Her lips encased him.

"A little lower," he encouraged.

She sank further down his shaft.

"Well done," he praised, "but there is much left."

She tried to take more of him, but barely took half an inch. He pressed her head down. Seconds later, she began to gag. He gave her a respite before placing his erection before her. She took in the same length before she began to convulse.

"I cannot!" she protested after coming off him. "It is far too long!"

"There is more than enough space in your throat."

Her eyes widened.

"You must relax your reflexes."

"Impossible."

"When you first attempted the Sonata in E-flat Major by Haydn, did you think that impossible?"

"No."

"Could you play it at first?"

"No."

"Then why did you not think it possible?"

"I knew mastering it required practice."

"And I take it you practiced."

He held his shaft for her. She opened her mouth. He allowed her to take what she could this time. His hand still fisted in her hair, he guided her mouth up and down his shaft.

"Mind your teeth," he reminded her.

Despite her discomfort, she made a concerted effort

to meet his rhythm. He dared to push a little deeper. She stiffened at first and coughed, but he did not withdraw.

"Breathe and relax," he said.

She closed her eyes, took a breath, and settled about his cock. He thrust himself into her. She did not suck as heartily as his mistress, but her mouth was still bloody delightful. He shoved his hips with increased vigor. A delicious agitation swirled in his groin, mounting in his cods, threatening to implode if it did not find escape. Trudie attempted to remain calm and tried to quell the gagging. He continued to push upon her head until she squirmed and sputtered, but her protests were muffled. His legs tensed, and with a roar, he released the tension coiled inside him. Wave after wave of his seed spilled forth. Her body heaved as if she retched. His seed dropped from her lips.

He shuddered several times before falling a step back. She spat and coughed. A tear slid down her cheek. His heart hammered in his chest as he stared at her. Thrice he had taken her mouth. In one night. And never would he have thought to ravish his wife's virginal mouth. When he had recovered his breath, he gave her cheek a pat.

"Well done, my wench. In the future, you will learn to swallow every drop. It will please your husband immensely." He was already more pleased than he should be. His attempt at schooling Trudie had turned into something more.

Chapter Thirteen

HOW WAS IT HE had never seen how wanton his wife could be?

Leopold remembered how her cheeks had blushed red as two tomatoes when he had first kissed her hand. They had not had much of a courtship. Having been indifferent to most women he had come across, Leopold had acquiesced to the marriage easily enough. Perhaps if he had taken the time to know Trudie better, he would have sensed this part of her.

But she was such a timid creature. If he had not asserted himself forcefully, her prurience might never have seen the light of day.

This thought tempered the ever present guilt of what he did.

He wiped a drop of his seed from the corner of her mouth and cupped her chin to raise her gaze to his. "Husbands may want an upstanding wife, virtuous and chaste, to parade before others; but in the bedchamber, they all want a harlot. I commend you for your willingness to be your husband's whore."

"I am not merely his," she replied with misery, lowering her lashes.

Guilt twisted in his groin.

"I think he will forgive the trespass once he sees how you have been changed."

"An easy statement for you to make, sir. You know not—how can any husband forgive adultery? And if he knew the extent of my treachery, the depths of my depravity, he would be more than ashamed."

"How well do you know your husband?"

"Our families have been close for generations."

"And you are thus privy to his most private inclinations, his thoughts and sentiments?"

Trudie became silent.

"If he were a man of such high character," he continued, "would your husband have taken a mistress? He spoke the same vows as you at the wedding, did he not?"

"Yes, but allowances are made for his sex."

"Should your sex not be afforded the same allowances?"

He realized his words betrayed his own hypocrisy. He had been furious with her infidelity but had spared little thought on the wrong he himself had committed.

Trudie shook her head. "Neither you nor my friend can convince me that what I do is acceptable."

"Then why do you submit yourself to me?"

"I know not. This Château has clouded my mind. I cannot think properly."

"Then let us dispense with thinking. It is the purpose of Château Follet to exalt the carnal, after all."

He reached between her legs and caressed her. She was still wet. He knelt on one knee and put a tongue to

127

her folds.

She gave a half cry, half laugh. "P-Please!"

He marveled once more at the sensitivity of her body before flicking his tongue over her pearl of pleasure.

She convulsed. "Oh, God! God!"

After inhaling her arousal, he pried apart her folds to gain better access at the delightful bud.

"No, no!"

"I think your body wishes to spend again, my naughty Jezebel."

She shook her head.

He licked at the swollen flesh, surprised she had not yet grown accustomed to the euphoria.

"Pray, it is too sensitive, sir," she whimpered.

But he continued to stroke her engorged pleasure bud.

"Please!" she begged.

He switched to ply his fingers against her. "Do you not wish to spend?"

"It is…it is always hard…at first."

"But a good student must spend when her master bids it."

"No…"

The blood had rushed to his groin, hardening his desire. He put a hand upon her back in an attempt to still her convulsing while he strummed her clitoris.

Stepping away from her, he watched her body quiver, at once wanting and dreading a return of his fondling. He waited to see if she would change her mind and ask him to continue caressing her instead.

He drew a teasing finger along her slit. She shivered violently and moaned.

Her eyes were wide, and he saw her confliction in her furrowed brow. She struggled not to want the natural desires of her body.

Reaching between her legs, he found a spot that made her cry out and her back arch, but she did not ask him to stop. She was as sensitive as ever, mayhap more, and copiously wet. As his fingers worked their torment, she emitted a strange litany of sounds from gasping to wailing to sobbing. Her body twisted, and she began to pant.

Sensing her peak near, he commanded, "Spend, my love, spend."

Her body quaked, fighting the impending eruption, but his fingers wrested from her that ultimate carnal bliss. She screamed as a paroxysm bowled into her. Arousal surged with satisfaction within him as he beheld her writhing and shaking. Till tonight, he had not known a woman to spend with ferocity.

He was in awe.

* * * * *

As she lay upon the bed, Leopold sat beside her and untied her. She lay immobile He rubbed her breasts, her legs, and her backside, enjoying the suppleness of her body. His member was stiff as a maypole and would need tending to.

After she had rested a while, he said, "On your feet. We will continue with your instruction."

She sat up and wrapped her arms over her bosom. "Instruction?"

"Did you not wish to be a good little whore for your husband?"

"I can take no more, sir. The hour must be late indeed."

"But we have hardly begun."

Her eyes widened.

"There is much to learn if you wish to please your husband."

"Is this really what would please him?"

"Men are simple creatures, and not a one would reject an offer to swallow his member."

She was silent, and he took this opportunity to caution her, "Perhaps you will not be so easily swayed by your friend in the future?"

"Perhaps she did not fully understand what transpires here."

He snorted. "Your friend was once a frequent guest."

Trudie glanced up. "You know her?" She searched his countenance, perhaps wanting to ask if he had been with Diana before. He had not, but he had known many of Diana's past lovers, some of whom were quite verbose with their escapades.

"She was never a lover of mine," he confirmed. "She has a cousin who once visited Château Follet as well."

She stared at him agog. Her voice wavered. "Her cousin? What was his—or her—name?"

"I prefer to respect the anonymity of the guests here."

"She has few cousins…"

He held out his hand. "I wish to show you another enjoyment of men."

Her mind obviously still whirled at the knowledge he had given her, but she accepted his hand. He rubbed his erection.

"What do you intend?" she asked.

He lay down. "Straddle me."

She knit her brows, perplexed.

"As you would a horse," he explained, taking her hand and pulling her to him.

She placed a knee beside him. He pulled her thigh across his pelvis till it rested beside his hip. He settled her over him before pointing his shaft at her quim.

"This is most awkward, sir," she mumbled, unable to meet his gaze.

"It is a divine position. Now ride me."

Hesitating, she adjusted herself over and over again till his patience thinned, and he pulled her thighs wide to lower her body.

"Sir!"

"Worry not. You shall enjoy it, as you have before."

He thrust his hips up and speared himself into her. She gave a loud gasp and attempted to wriggle off him, but he held her in place. Her wet heat was glorious.

"Ride," he instructed.

"But how——?"

He demonstrated by lifting her till she came to the tip of his cock, then pulling her down by the hips till she encased his entire length.

"Up and down," he said. "As if you were riding a horse."

He assisted the motions till she had a sense of the rhythm. Releasing her, he watched as her breasts bounded up and down. His erection was already hard as could be. He could have spent then and there if he lacked control.

"My legs grow sore, sir," she complained.

"I did not give you leave to stop."

He reached up and grasped both breasts with his hands. Soon perspiration dampened her body. Her brow furrowed as she grunted and panted.

"I cannot…it is too difficult to continue," she pleaded.

He gripped her hips and shoved himself into her till her teeth chattered. Tension fisted in his groin, his release near. Just before the boiling in his cods threatened to spill over, he pushed her off of him, came onto his knees, and allowed his mettle to rain upon her belly. He bucked his hips several times till the last of his seed had dropped. With a shake of his head, he fell beside her on the bed.

"Well done, my love," he said between ragged breaths. "I vow your husband would be proud."

Chapter Fourteen

SHE HAD SURELY DESCENDED to a level within hell, Trudie thought to herself as she lay upon the bed and stared up at the ceiling. Her debaucher, having spent, lay beside her, breathing hard.

Your husband would be proud, he had said after he had spilled his seed upon her.

Was such a thing possible? Could Leopold be proud? Not of her infidelity. Of that she was certain he would be furious—or worse, devastated. She tried not to think on that and instead replayed her acts of wantonness. If she had taken Leopold into her mouth as she had done with the masked stranger beside her, if she straddled her husband and rode him, would that have been enough to stay him from straying?

It mattered not if it would. For in coming to Château Follet with her husband's cousin, Diana, she had allowed herself to be seduced and committed a transgression in the most depraved and wanton manner. The night had devolved from caresses to a dark torment. She had submitted to such things that would have appalled herself but yesterday.

"You think overmuch, madam."

"I am merely...fatigued," she prevaricated. Her head

did still feel foggy, but that was likely due to the champagne. And it was perhaps a lack of sufficient thinking that had landed her in her current predicament.

He rose from the bed and went to ring the servant's bell. At that, she sat up and reached for the bedlinen.

"I did not allow you could cover yourself," he said whilst he pulled on his breeches.

She looked down at his drying mettle upon her belly. "May I at least cleanse myself?"

He grinned. "I like the look of my mark upon you."

She flushed. "You delight in wantonness."

"It is part of the allure here."

"For you."

"Have you not been aroused?"

She could not deny she had.

"Arousal is an odd beast to which there are many paths," he continued. "Here at Château Follet, the titillation is driven by the more wanton, the more depraved and wrong."

"It does not have to be so."

"You did not have to come here."

His tone had an edge.

"I did not—my friend did not fully inform me of what transpires here!"

"Yes, it was mischievous of her not to have told you everything," he considered with a frown, as if he were displeased with Diana somehow, though Trudie could not imagine why. What did a stranger care how Diana conducted herself? Certainly he had profited from Diana's waywardness.

"Nevertheless," he continued, "I wonder that she would have brought you here lest she had some indication that you would take to the activities."

Her mouth dropped. "I would never have given her any evidence to support such a thing!" She had not known it herself.

"Perhaps not knowingly—"

"I have ever only been truthful and honest with her."

"Indeed?"

She furrowed her brow. Why was he questioning her relationship with Diana?

"As truthful and honest as you have been with your husband?"

Her bottom lip quivered, and he shifted—in discomfort, it seemed. She said in a small voice, "Till now, yes. I had been a good wife—or so I thought. Perhaps not an adequate wife. But I was honest, and kind, and virtuous. Now none of that matters. I am the opposite of all that."

He gazed downward till a knock at the door roused him. It was a maid. Trudie pulled the bedlinen over her.

"Bring up some tea," he told the maid. After glancing at Trudie, he added, "and some biscuits. With strawberry jam."

Trudie perked up. She often enjoyed a dollop of strawberry jam on her biscuits.

After the maid departed, he closed the door and turned to Trudie. She quickly uncovered herself, then blushed as if she had not been naked before him already. She felt his gaze caress every curve of her body.

"You say you have been a virtuous wife," he remarked.

"Had been," she murmured with eyes downcast.

"Perhaps that is why you are drawn to Follet. It is an opportunity to be naughty. Under the weight of virtue, of being the good, diligent, upstanding wife, the pendulum has swung the other way."

"That is no vindication, sir, for what I have done."

"I did not intend it for a defense, merely an explanation that is less damning and more forgiving of human nature."

"I could never forgive myself."

Her voice wavered, and she feared she might cry.

"What if your husband forgave you, could you forgive yourself then?"

She stared at him as if he were mad. "What husband would forgive his wife the crime of adultery?"

"You said he was guilty first. You, at the least, are paying a form of penance, albeit a pleasurable one."

Again, she turned crimson. "It is not always pleasurable."

"No?"

Her heartbeat skittered when he approached the bed. He removed the sash of his banyan.

"Please," she pleaded, though she knew not what he intended. "Have we not done enough?"

"We had an agreement. Present your wrists."

She stared at the sash pulled taut between his hands. She considered running away, but he would catch her, as he had in the music room, and be vexed.

Reluctantly, she presented her wrists. He bound them together with one end of the sash, then tied the other end to a cornice atop the headboard. Sitting beside her upon the bed, he reached for her thighs.

"What do you intend?" she asked, though she knew his hand's destination.

"To prove that while you may not have relished every minute of what has transpired, pleasure endures."

She watched his hand slide between her legs and groaned when his digits brushed the slick flesh there.

"As it would for any good wench," he whispered in her ear, his words taunting and tantalizing.

She shook her head in feeble protest.

"You have acknowledged yourself a harlot," he said, lightly stroking her. "Exalt in your admission. Is it not better than being a virtuous wife?"

"Nooo…"

She shut her eyes at his invasive fondling and how they lighted the most thrilling sensations.

"Many a woman would be done for the evening," he continued, "but harlots are rarely satiated, their bodies forever greedy to spend."

She could only whimper, trying not to mind how his fingers slid against her, grazing that nub of desire. A moan escaped her lips.

"It is a shame your husband knew naught of your wanton nature. I vow he would have enjoyed it."

Was that possible? She half-wondered. The other half of her mind could not escape his ministrations.

There was still dampness there, allowing his fingers to glide easily along her.

"You know not my husband," she said, hoping discourse would stall her arousal. "It pleases you to project your own inclinations onto him."

"At their core, men are not such diverse creatures. I know your husband—or his sort—better than you think. Can you not imagine him caressing you as I do now?"

"I think not."

"Why not?"

"My husband has not come into my bed for some time."

"And you wish he would?"

Yes. And no. She had no wish to repeat the awkwardness and the discomfort of their marriage night. If she could be assured of his desire and her ability to enjoy his touch, she would desire greatly to share her bed with him.

When she made no reply, he pressed, "Or do you doubt he could please you?"

"You are impertinent to ask such questions, sir."

Shifting her hips, she tried unsuccessfully to escape his probing hand. He pinched her clitoris, making her yelp.

"Perhaps you doubt his skills as a lover."

"It is not something I considered! I have no particular expectations…"

"Why not?"

"Because he is my husband. I would accept him if

he lacked any skills. For certain, I would not have been the wiser as I have no basis to draw a comparison."

His fingers plied the spots that made her shiver. "Till now."

Till now, she agreed.

"Would it please you if he could do what I do to you?"

That familiar ache had begun unfurling in her loins, making her breath uneven, making her body tremble and tense.

"No," she exhaled.

He withdrew his hand. Her body strained toward him, no longer fearful of the sensations his stroking elicited. He cupped a breast. She groaned, glad for the touch but aggravated that he did not apply it to a path that could lead to her desired destination.

"You deceive yourself, madam."

He brushed his thumb over a nipple before tugging on the stiff bud. The ache between her legs throbbed.

A knock at the door indicated the maid had returned. He rose from the bed.

"Wait!" Trudie cried, tugging at her bonds.

"Stay as you are," he replied before walking to the door.

"But—"

He received the tea try from the maid and went to set it upon the table. He then returned to untie her wrists. She sat up.

Returning to the table where the tea had been set, he pulled out a chair. She thought of asking to dress first, but when he handed her his banyan, she knew he did not expect her to attire herself. With a difficult swallow and as the agitation his hand had provoked still swirled below her belly, she grudgingly rose from the bed, slipped into the robe, and went to sit at the table.

He added a little milk to the tea he poured, as she liked it, before handing her the cup. She found the heat of the tea comforting. He placed the plate of biscuits and the jam before her.

"Thank you," she said, taking a biscuit and trying to find normalcy in taking tea with a masked stranger whilst she sat in naught but a robe. She pressed her thighs together in an attempt to ease the pressure. Had he forgotten the state he had left her in? Or was it his intention to leave her body bereft?

Of course it was deliberate.

He seemed always to act with intention. A part of her hated him for this, for tormenting her with equal parts pain and pleasure. Yet, she could not bring herself to think him pure evil, as much as she wanted to. Perhaps it was because she had heard, at times, pity in his voice. At other times, she heard anger—more anger at her than was warranted, for she was a stranger to him.

Something he had said earlier returned to her, and she wanted to break the silence between them. The longer they sat, the more conscious she became of her nakedness.

He had pulled his chair away from the table to give him room to cross his legs. He had finished his first cup and did not partake of the biscuits or jam.

"You had asked," she ventured as she nibbled upon a biscuit, "if I could forgive myself if my husband did. Do you think a man—any man—capable of forgiving the crime of adultery?"

"Your husband is Christian, is he not?"

"I did not speak of my husband."

"Your hypothetical is of no use if it does not address your husband."

He sounded rather grim when he spoke the word 'husband.'

"Of course he is Christian, though perhaps he does not attend church as regularly as he ought."

"I presume he attended often enough to know that forgiveness is a Christian value."

"But adultery is among the worst of sins."

"Does John not say that if we confess our sins, He is faithful and just to forgive us our sins and cleanse us of all unrighteousness?"

"That does not give us license to do whatever we will. And whilst the Lord might forgive, my husband may not."

He looked down in thought for a moment before saying, "Do you forgive your husband?"

At first, she could not answer for she had not asked herself this. "I do not fault him," she thought aloud. "My husband could have had a much prettier, much wittier woman than I had he not felt obligated to offer his hand to me. I think I was a wretched disappointment on our wedding night."

"Wedding nights are far easier for the groom."

"Yes, but I think I frightened him with my sobbing. I had not—I had not expected it would hurt as much as it did. He tried—I believe he tried to make it pleasurable for me."

"Tried and failed."

"I am certain the experience contributed to his desire to seek a mistress. Had I not been in such hysterics, had I been—I did not think I could derive pleasure from the venereal. I was convinced my body was not inclined to it."

"But it is. I would say exceedingly so."

Blushing, she stared into her tea. "Had I known...well, perhaps it would not have made a difference to Leopold."

"Are you so certain?"

She blinked several times in thought. "Yes. No. How can one be certain? Regardless, he has a mistress now."

Silence fell between them again till he spoke.

"Earlier this evening you had remarked that it was not uncommon for husbands to take mistresses, but that does not mean you condone it."

She took another biscuit and put a dollop of jam upon it. The tea and sustenance seemed to help settle her nerves.

"I do not," she acknowledged.

"And while you say that you do not fault your husband for his infidelity, that is not the same as forgiveness."

"Luke says, 'If your brother sins, rebuke him, and if

he repents, forgive him, and if he sins against you seven times in the day, and turns to you seven times, saying, "I repent", you must forgive him.'"

"It is easy to quote scripture, but much harder to follow it."

"Yes," she agreed. How was it she had fallen into such easy conversation about so delicate a matter with this stranger?

After another minute of silence, he said, "I would hazard you have not forgiven him or you would not have come to Château Follet."

"Perhaps. I suppose I must forgive him now if I hope to have his forgiveness."

"Do you?"

"Do I what?"

"He knows not that you are here. He might never discover that you came here."

"Are you suggesting I deceive him?"

"Do you intend to inform him?"

"I could not live with such a deception! To look him in the eye, day after day, knowing what I have done—I could not!"

"Then you are a better person than most," he said wryly.

The acts of depravity had stayed her mind from having to think on the consequences of her actions, but now that the subject had come up, she felt ill at ease

* * * * *

143

"I would finish what I had started," he said after they had finished the tea. He pointed to the ground before him. She knelt in front of him.

"Good little wanton," he whispered into her ear.

He cradled a breast and appeared to admire how it spilled over his fingers. He stroked the side of the orb with his thumb before reaching over to tug at her nipple. He rolled the nub and pinched it. She grunted and felt her body begin to melt into the heat of desire.

"Touch yourself," he instructed.

Without protest, she complied, thrusting her hand between her thighs. He continued to play with her nipple as she stroked. What a wanton indeed she had become!

"You are a lovely sight when you pleasure yourself."

He alternated between breasts while she slid her fingers against herself. She wanted to press both breasts into his hands. He knelt before her, close enough for her nipples to touch his chest. He pushed and groped both orbs, pulled and pinched her nipples till she whimpered. Then he cupped her face with both hands and brought his lips down upon hers. How she wished Leopold would kiss her so!

"Remember not to spend till I have permitted it," he murmured against her mouth.

Her reply was muffled by the kiss. She marveled at how much she enjoyed the locking of their lips, as much as she delighted in his other caresses. It felt as if, through her mouth, he intended to possess all of her. When he parted from her and his hands slid from her

SURRENDERING TO THE BARON

face, she groaned a little.

He stood and watched her fondle herself. She circled the nub between her folds, wondering what her reward would be. As the tension between her legs grew, she closed her eyes.

"Enough," he commanded.

She was reluctant and relieved to cease her ministrations. "Come."

He lifted her, turned her around and positioned her above his lap. Her debaucher sank Trudie onto his shaft, filling her aching cunnie. She shut her eyes because the sensation was too marvelous. Her body had longed for this.

Trudie trembled and yelped as her arousal drilled deep into her belly with every stroke, every throb inside of her. The wave was cresting. She cried out.

The spasms nearly knocked her from his lap, but he embraced her with his other arm, holding onto her tight. She shook against him and sobbed for air as she drowned in bliss.

He bucked his hips at her, and soon she felt the heat of his seed inside her as he roared and his body shook. If she were not wallowing in rapture still, she might have begun to panic. She collapsed against his chest, calmed by his deep breathing. He kissed her temple with a rare tenderness.

Chapter Fifteen

WHEN TRUDIE EMERGED FROM her daze, she tried to slip from him, but Leopold enjoyed having her upon his lap.

"Stay," he directed, holding onto her.

She resisted.

"Stay yourself, madam."

His stern tone jolted her to obey.. He reached around her and cupped a breast. She stiffened and shivered. He squeezed and kneaded the ample flesh in his hand. Lust stirred in his groin. Good God, could he possibly spend again? Till now, the most he had spent in the span of four and twenty hours was thrice. He had lost count of how many times he had made Trudie spend.

"Did you know your body was so favorably given to spending?" he asked her, dropping his hand from her breast to her crotch. His fingers toyed with the patch of hair there.

Her voice quivered. "No."

"It is a shame your husband was unaware of this most lovely attribute."

"I—I do not think that would matter."

"You underestimate your appeal. What husband

would not desire a wife who spends as lovely as you do?" He reached for the flesh beneath her curls.

"You need not be so complimentary."

With her countenance turned away, he could not see her expression, but he thought he heard a hitch when she spoke.

"I assure you your husband would be much impressed."

"You can assure this? Do you know him?"

She seemed to accuse him.

"I know he must be an incompetent lover for you to have risked coming here."

"Alas, I was not the most encouraging when it came to…the marital bed."

"He should not have given up so easily."

"I knew not my body was capable of…"

"Perhaps you would have made this discovery sooner if your husband possessed my skills."

She stiffened.

"Do you wish your husband had my skills? Would it please you to have him bind you to the bed and wrest the rapture from your body as I have?"

She was quiet before answering, "Better my husband than any other man."

"You must not rue your time with me. I send you back to your husband a better woman."

She made a strange sound. He dipped his fingers between her folds. Upon connecting with the wetness there, he felt the blood course more strongly through him. She clamped her thighs together and squirmed from his touch.

"Do you not wish for your reward?" he asked.

"I think not."

"Resistance is futile now that you have come this far." He forced his hand to her quim. "Note how copiously wet you are."

"That is—that is not all my—but your—you spent *inside me.*"

And it was glorious, but he understood her concerns. "Do you fear you will conceive?"

She tried to wriggle from his probing fingers. "Have you no care for what you might have done? Of how you might have ruined me?"

The anguish in her voice gave him pause. In his time at Château Follet, he had always had French letters at the ready for when he wished to spill his seed inside a woman, but as Trudie was his wife, it was not necessary. But she knew not this.

"What would you do if you were with child—my child?"

She moaned. "Do not ask such a thing!"

"Would you pass the child off as his?"

At that, she tried to slide off his lap, but he fisted his other hand in her hair and held her in place. She cried out but remained where she was. He resumed fondling her between the legs, encouraging the rosebud there to protrude.

"Would you?" he pressed.

"How dare you ask such an odious question!"

He admitted it was in poor form, but he was

curious. He pinched her rosebud. "Answer me."

"How could I? It were not possible!"

Her lack of easy pretense gratified him. He had previously found her naivete rather dull, but her artlessness was now refreshing. He decided to provide her a solution.

"It is quite easy, madam. Simply spread your legs beneath your husband as you have done for me. Do this upon your return home and he will be none the wiser."

She renewed her struggles. The shifting of her body atop him made him harden with lust. He sank two curled fingers into her and found a spot within that made her gasp and tremble.

"And if he hesitates to take you, you have but to make the pretty noises you make now, and he will want nothing else but to fuck you."

"Oh…God…" she panted as her legs shook. "…Stop…"

When she tried to slide once more off him, he pulled her down to him. Her head fell against his chest. A range of emotions swarmed within him: arousal, anger, gratitude, guilt. He was undecided if he welcomed her coming to Château Follet. At first, he had considered it nothing but awful. But then he had seen a part of her he would never have known existed. Though her intended infidelity enraged him, he was also glad not to be the only guilty party.

He stroked her and watched as her eyes rolled toward the back of her head before she shut her eyes.

"Please," she whined. "No more. I am done."

"Your body contradicts you. I think it would readily spend again."

Her eyes flew open. "No!"

"There is no virtue in resisting. You have taken my member into your mouth and allowed me to spend within you—"

She grabbed the hand between her legs. "I did not! I did not know you would take such a liberty!"

Trudie was not practiced in such circumstances. The advantage had always been his, and he had not hesitated to press it.

"I beg your pardon," he said.

"I won't!"

He stopped. The force of her words surprised him. "Won't what?"

"I won't pardon you!"

"As I've said, your husband need not be the wiser."

"But *I* am the wiser. I could not perpetrate a deceit such as you have described."

"You would confess the truth to him?"

He saw the agony in her eyes and cursed himself for a blackguard.

"I would," she whispered.

He believed her, and for a moment, he felt unworthy of her honesty.

"Is your husband deserving of your honesty?" he challenged, now vexed that she seemed to hold the superior moral standing though it was she who had come to the Château seeking to commit adultery.

"It matters not. I could not bring myself—I have

not the wherewithal to carry on a deception that would require me to live a lie every day of my life!"

"But you have already deceived him in coming here."

"Yes, but…I had not thought—I would not have sinned had I not crossed paths with you!"

He recalled her resistance earlier in the night, which now felt like days ago. It was true he had forced himself upon her, but surely she was not all reluctance for she had spent at his hand?

"You bear no fault?" he returned.

"I did not say that. I have been complicit enough in my sin and shall rue it till the day I die."

He scoffed, "That is a theatrical approach you need not take. You have merely equaled his infidelity, and if he is none the wiser—provided your friend, Diana, is discreet—"

"I could not bear it if he were to learn from another! I must tell him myself…"

For a moment, he sat stunned before asking, "You mean to confess to your husband?"

"I must," she answered slowly. "I could not harbor such a secret such as this. It would eat at my soul."

Hearing the misery in her voice, he put a hand to his head and tried to fight back the guilt. He had felt only a small amount of remorse for hiding his mistress from Trudie because his motivations had been kind. He had thought to shelter Trudie from the pain of his faithlessness.

"And how do you think your husband will receive

your confession?"

"He will be livid. Furious."

"Then why confess? Is it to satisfy to your own conscience?"

She lowered her eyes.

"Or perhaps he will be relieved," he offered.

"No. No husband would be anything but affronted and vexed to be made a cuckold. Only...you knew Diana from before. Did you also know my husband?"

He had eschewed her earlier question of the same. "Not everyone reveals his identity at Château Follet. I may have crossed his path and not know it. But why do you think I would know your husband?"

"Diana..."

His jaw tightened. "Your friend told you?"

"Not in words, but you had said her cousin was a patron here. My husband is the only cousin of hers I know of ...Pray tell me, was my husband—has my husband been here before?"

He drew in several silent breaths as he debated the response he wanted to give.

"Yes," he answered.

Chapter Sixteen

LEOPOLD COULD SEE THAT Trudie was stunned. He allowed the newfound knowledge time to sink in for her. In his revelation, he had hoped to ameliorate some of her self-reproach.

She broke the silence by asking, "Did he come with his mistress?"

"He was a guest many years ago," he replied. "I do not think he has returned since."

"But how would you know?"

"He strikes me as the sort of man who does not take matrimony lightly. He would have made an attempt to be the honorable husband, but you would know better."

She shook her head. "I think I hardly know him at all."

He swallowed the guilt that threatened to rise in his bile. He moved the hand that remained between her thighs, startling her. "Did I not say I would return you to your husband a better wife?"

He stroked her gently, but she resumed her earlier resistance. The wriggling of her arse upon his lap woke the lust that had cooled during their dialogue.

"Please—" she demurred.

"I seek only to pleasure you. You need not worry

that you will have to attend me."

"I am overcome. I can hardly think—"

He brushed his fingers against her folds. "Spending can clear the mind."

Her hesitation was all he needed to continue. He stroked her clitoris and breathed in the arousal emanating from between her legs. He murmured in her hair, "Come, you have earned this."

"I have not."

"I command you to spend for me."

She groaned, "Have I not done all that you have asked?"

"What purpose does denying yourself serve?"

"Perhaps I could take your—take you into my mouth one last time?"

"I much prefer to see you spend. It is a thing of beauty."

"Have mercy on a wretched soul, sir."

"One last time and I shall set you free."

"Only once more?"

"Once more."

Taking her silence as acquiescence, he sank his digits into her hot, wet cunnie. She gasped when he curled his fingers and stroked her, making her shiver from head to toe. When he felt certain she would not try to escape, he dropped his other hand to her breast, rolled the orb and gently tugged at the nipple. With a moan, she closed her eyes and surrendered. No longer angry at the fact that his wife writhed beneath the hands of a man she thought a stranger, he sought only her pleasure. With his hands, he coaxed her to that ultimate carnal bliss, relishing her every sigh and purr, the flow of wetness between her thighs, and the rise and fall of her bosom.

But his forbearance could only withstand so much. Her squirming and panting, the flutter of her lashes, her naked form all conspired to lend his lust the upper hand. He ground his groin against her bottom. His strength of will crumbled.

In one motion, he stood and bent her over the chair. She yelped in surprise. "What do you—" she began.

He positioned himself behind her, taking in the fullness of her arse rounding the edge of the seat. Reaching around her hip, he returned his hand between her thighs, fondling her till her breath grew shaky. He rubbed his shaft between the cheeks of her derrière. Angling his shaft lower, he thrust into her.

"No! Wait—"

Her objection turned into a long low moan as his fingers strummed her wet flesh. Over and over, she groaned while he bucked his hips, slapping his pelvis into her rump.

"Such a good wench," he muttered, his thrusting causing the chair to scrape against the ground.

"Please don't spend—oh—my—God," she babbled.

He dared to thrust harder. Her tightness was exquisite. The way the flesh of her arse quivered, the heat and wetness encasing his shaft, the sound of flesh against flesh—he was near to spending himself. A cry burst from her lips, and her body began convulsing atop the chair. Her cunnie clenched, and he lost control. The tension in his groin unraveled and spilled into her. With a groan, he speared himself deeper into her as spasms wracking his body. He pumped himself into her, claiming her through his release.

Collapsing onto her back, he remained inside of her until his cock became flaccid and slid from her of its own accord. He kissed her between the shoulder blades. "My dear, you are marvelous."

She made no sound, but when he drew her up from the chair, she turned around and began to pommel him.

"You brute!" she cried.

He grabbed her wrists. What the devil was wrong with her?

She continued her efforts to assault him, though he easily restrained her.

"You spent!" she accused. "*Inside* me! *Again*."

Her reaction baffled him for she had not erupted in such a manner in the Orange Room.

"Calm yourself," he said. "I assure you, you have nothing to worry of."

Capitulating to his superior strength, she sank to her knees. He replaced his fall and looked upon her as she hung her head. He dropped to a knee before her.

"My dear, you fret needlessly."

She lifted her head and glared at him through what appeared to be tears. "You selfish bastard!"

"Nothing will come of it."

"How can you be certain?"

"Why torment yourself with what may not come to pass?"

"Torment? Yes, it will be a daily torment until— what if—what if the worst—but you do not have to suffer the consequences! You may indulge in being a selfish rogue without penalty."

The pain in her countenance cut at him, and her words were salt upon the wounds. He reached to put a comforting hand upon her, but she swiped him away.

"Touch me not," she seethed.

The vehemence in her voice surprised him. Until now, she had been the nervous and timid Trudie he had always known.

"Did I not provide a solution—" he began.

"You wish me to mislead my husband? I told you I could not! I would not deceive him into raising another man's child."

"Does your husband not need an heir?"

His response seemed to stun her. She gave a cry and lunged at him. He caught her wrists.

"Trudie!"

The sound of her name stayed her. Eyes wide, she retreated from him.

"I promise you that all will be well," he assured.

"How…?"

He knew not whether she asked how he knew all would be well or how he knew her name. Either way, there was but one way to allay her fears.

He removed his mask.

* * * * *

Her hands flew to her mouth, stifling her scream. He cursed in silence to see the horror upon her features.

"You see now that there was no reason for your distress," he said, hoping relief would soon manifest for her.

Her bosom heaved and her hands trembled as she continued to stare wordlessly at him.

"And the sin which you thought to have committed never took place."

When she made no response, he began to wonder if she had heard him. He bridged the distance between them and reached for her, but she shied away from him.

"Trudie…"

To his surprise, she shook her head vigorously, brushed past him and was out the chamber.

Chapter Seventeen

Two Months Later ~

WILL YOU NEVER FORGIVE him?" Diana asked as the two strolled the small garden behind the home of Mrs. Atwood, a longtime friend of Trudie's mother and whom she had been staying with for the past two months. After leaving Château Debauchery, Trudie had not returned home.

"It is Christian to forgive," Trudie replied as she watched a robin fly from its perch in a birch tree.

"But I think you have not forgiven Leopold or you would have returned to him. Did you receive the letters of his I forwarded?"

"I did."

"And did you respond to any of them?"

"No."

Diana heaved a sigh.

"I hope you did not inform him of where I was?" Trudie worried.

"Of course not. I betrayed your trust once. I could not do it again."

Trudie bit her lower lip, feeling sorry for the pain upon her friend's countenance.

She had forgiven Diana for concealing the fact that Leopold had once been a frequent guest of Château Follett, but it was true that she had not completely forgiven her husband for his deception. She had come close many times, having spent many sleepless nights oscillating between remorse, guilt, anger, and sorrow. She understood Leopold had come to Château Follett in disguise so that he could observe her faithfulness, or lack thereof. And she had failed him.

No matter that her paramour had turned out to be her own husband. He had been known to her only as a stranger. And she had succumbed to this 'stranger.' Not once, but over and over again. She had spent for her debaucher in ways she had never done with her husband. She was guilty of a terrible sin, and no excuse could exonerate her.

She had overcome her anguish at Leopold for such acts of depravity that would surely send her to hell because the wanton part of her did find titillation in the wicked acts. Recalling them, she would often find herself aroused and needing to touch the parts of her body his fingers and mouth had kissed. Not only had she discovered, at last, that carnal euphoria she had envied in Diana whenever her friend spoke of it, she had felt relieved that she could find pleasure in her body, that she was not doomed to forever recoil at the thought of congress with her husband. Perhaps, then, she should be thankful that she had been liberated from her prior shackles.

She had even felt desired. Seeing the lust burn in the

eyes of her debaucher, she had felt emboldened, even beautiful. That man had wanted her. He had grown hard for her. And that man was Leopold. The discovery ought to have thrilled her to no end. Because she had never thought it possible.

It was her own doing. Had she not come to Château Follett in the first place, none of this would have come to pass. She would still be the faithful wife, quietly enduring the fact that Leopold had a mistress whom he desired more than his wife. Did she truly want such an existence? It was clear that at Château Follett, she had pleased him greatly when she had doubted she ever could. At most, Leopold would tolerate her. Was she not, then, improved in some manner as a result of Château Follet?

But the pain she had felt, when she had thought she could be with child and was tortured by the pain, disappointment, outrage that such a revelation must cause her husband, proved too much still. How could Leopold have allowed her to wallow in such agony when he knew the truth? Did he not believe the sincerity of her pain? Did he not care to lift her misery?

But he had or he would not have revealed himself.

Diana sighed. "I feel I am to blame. I have made matters worse between you and Leopold."

"I was unhappy in my marriage," Trudie replied. "That would only have continued. And I could not make peace with it or I would not have come to Château Follett with you."

"It is kind of you to say so, but who knows, Leopold

might have tired of his mistress and returned to your waiting arms."

"You must not torment yourself with such thoughts. They shall never bear fruit, or not of a good sort."

"You have come to accept what had happened then?"

"I have accepted that I cannot change the past."

"And what do you intend for the future?"

It was a question she had no answer for. "What do you? Does your husband still know nothing of Château Follett?"

"I thought for certain Leopold would tell Charles. He was plenty furious at me for having brought you to Château Follett. But I think he was too grieved over what had transpired betwixt you two that the part I played was a secondary concern for him. How much longer do you intend to make him suffer?"

"It is not my intention to make him suffer at all."

"Then why do you not answer his letters?"

"Because I have not yet read them."

Diana stopped in her tracks and stared wide-eyed at Trudie. "What? Not a one?"

Trudie looked up at the clouds in the sky. "I thought the wounds made by Château Follett should heal before I am ready to read his letters."

"Are they much healed or near to healed?"

Trudie dropped her gaze to the ground. "Do you know if Leopold has returned to his mistress?"

"He has not."

"How can you be certain?"

"I'm fairly certain. He asks of you almost daily. And when I was at the opera a fortnight ago, I saw her in the box of another gentleman, engaged in heavy flirtation with him."

Trudie released the breath she had not realized she had been holding. She found comfort in the news, though she believed she would not have reproached Leopold for returning to his mistress, especially after his wife had committed adultery. Perhaps she should not have run away from Château Follett. But she had been consumed too much by her own shame, by confusion, and horror at what she had done and what he had done. She had managed to make it to a posting inn and took the first available post-chaise to a destination she knew not nor cared not. At the end of the day, she found herself in the county where Mrs. Atwood resided. The woman had been much surprised to find Trudie at her door, but the kindly widow could plainly see that something was amiss and welcomed Trudie with much warmth and tenderness. She had made gentle inquiries, but when Trudie offered little explanation, Mrs. Atwood did not pry. Trudie had not intended to stay a two-month. She had trespassed upon Mrs. Atwood's hospitality long enough. But as time lengthened, she found it more and more difficult to return home, to confront her husband.

"I think you'll find Leopold a changed man," Diana said.

"In what manner?"

"I am fairly certain he regrets his actions, his

163

charade."

"He said as much?"

"No," Diana admitted as they resumed walking. "He won't speak to me of it, but I can see it in his eyes. I know that he has been everywhere looking for you. He tried not to worry your family and friends, but it could not be helped if you were to be found."

"And it is for that reason that I wrote to you."

"I am grateful—most grateful—that I have not lost your friendship and affection. But if I could forsake a part of it to earn your forgiveness of Leopold, I would."

Trudie could not help but be touched. "I shall find it in my heart to forgive Leopold. It is only a question of when, but I shall endeavor to make it sooner rather than later."

That appeared to satisfy Diana, and they finished their stroll with few words between them but full of patient understanding.

When Diana departed, Trudie was sad to see her friend leave. She saw that Diana had left her parasol behind. Holding the parasol, she decided that she would return it to her friend soon. Diana was in town, where Leopold was as well.

Trudie went into her chamber and opened the box containing his letters. She had locked them away as if by doing so, she could lock away and forget what had happened at Château Follet. But as much as she could not change the past, she could not forget it. Was she be ready for the flood of emotions that would surely drown her when she read his letters? Would she find his tone furious or contrite? It was possible both would engender from her the same reaction. Perhaps she had not forgiven Leopold because she had not forgiven herself.

She heard the wheels of a carriage outside. Diana had remembered her parasol. Grabbing it, Trudie hurried downstairs.

"You have a guest, Madame," the butler informed.

"Yes, thank you," she replied.

But stepping into the foyer, she froze. It was not Diana.

It was Leopold.

Chapter Eighteen

LEOPOLD TOOK IN TRUDIE'S trembling lower lip. She had lost weight for her cheeks had not their prior fullness and her arms had thinned. Her gown, with its empire waist, hid her form for the most part, but he hoped her hips, belly, thighs and arse—all the parts he had come to appreciate in their time at Château Follet—had not lost their suppleness.

Regardless, he found she looked quite lovely.

"I cannot believe that Diana betrayed me," Trudie whispered.

They stood the length of the foyer from one another. Having come on horseback, he was still in his riding clothes and likely smelled of horse, but given the circumstances, he had not the time to change to present himself properly.

"She did not," he told her. "I followed her without her knowledge."

He wanted to quip that it was gratifying how, in allowing Diana to visit her, Trudie trusted his cousin more than she trusted her husband, but he had no right to such sarcasm.

Sensing that Trudie, like a cornered mouse, wanted

to flee, he said gently, "As I am an uninvited guest here, I will not tarry, but would you grace me with your presence for a walk about the garden?"

She lowered her eyes in thought and fidgeted with her fingers. He hoped his assurance that he would not stay would mollify her, but he discerned resistance.

"A brief walk," he added.

Looking up, she met his gaze. "A brief walk."

She went to retrieve her bonnet and shawl. Upon her return, he would have offered his arm, but he assumed she would not wish to take it. Strolling past him, she headed to the garden. They ambled in silence for several minutes. He looked mostly at her while she looked mostly at the flowers, the sky, and her feet.

Finally, he said, "I begin to think no apology great enough to merit your forgiveness."

She said nothing.

"But one such could be had," he continued, "I would give it in any form you wish, as often as you wish."

She drew in a long breath as she stared at a bed of flowers. "I too am sorry. But apologies cannot undo the past."

He kept his gaze upon her. "No, they cannot. But they can pave the future."

"The future," she echoed with uncertainty.

When she said nothing further, he said, "Yes. You cannot expect to hide away here for the rest of time. You are still my wife."

Her back straightened. He refrained from pointing

out that, as her husband, he had the prerogative to dictate where she resided.

"I will overlook the fact that you have kept your whereabouts secret from me," he said, "though, as your husband, I have a right to know where you are. But I understand that what happened at Château Follet has caused you no small amount of distress."

She whirled around to face him. "No small amount of distress, sir? I wonder how many wives have suffered what I had?"

"And how many husbands would have banished their wives to a life of poverty for committing adultery?"

Her chest rose and her eyes widened. "Is that what you wish to do?"

He stared deep into her eyes. "I did not mean to threaten you."

"Certainly I deserve to be banished," she said, her voice cracking. "If that is what you wish—"

He grasped her by the arm, more tightly than he intended. "I have no such wish. I will not say that the thought never crossed my mind in my angrier moments, but I could not punish you in such a fashion when I was the first to sin."

She stared at his arm upon her. He could not make out what she felt, so he dropped his hold and retreated a step.

"Your sense of fairness is appreciated," she acknowledged.

The lack of emotion in her tone riled him. Fairness be damned.

"What I wish," he stated as calmly as he could, "is for us to move toward forgiveness. You have had ample time to consider it."

"You wish for me to forgive you for your deception, for the agony you caused me?"

"Yes, and I will forgive your being unfaithful."

"I did not lay with a man not my husband."

"No, but you would have if I had not been there."

"I would not have!"

He took a step toward her. "I sought to test you. Do you disavow that you failed?"

She looked down.

"You committed adultery in your heart. No court would absolve the intentions you held."

"What I did was wrong," she murmured. "I was wrong to repay your wrong with mine own, and your deception with mine. For that I am sorry."

He felt the pressure about his chest decrease. A part of him wanted to reach once more for her, but he did not wish to alarm her.

She looked up at him. "We ought not have married, you and I. Though it was the strongest wish of our families, we are not suited."

Why did she dwell on what could not be changed? he was about to challenge.

"I would not censure you if you wished to have nothing more to do with me," she said.

"Quite the contrary," he disputed. "I expect you to return with me to London tomorrow."

She was taken aback. "I had no intention of leaving.

Mrs. Atwood has graciously allowed me to stay for as long as I wish."

"With due respect to Mrs. Atwood and her hospitality, I mean to take my wife home."

"But I have no wish to return to London!"

"How much longer did you intend to stay here?"

"I know not, but I certainly am not prepared to leave on the morrow."

"You have stayed here long enough."

"That is your opinion, but I differ—"

"Prolonging your duration here would serve no purpose."

"You have no assurance of that. Pray do not lord over me as if we were at Château Follet!"

With another step, he closed the distance between them. He stared down at her intently, noting her breath had become uneven. "You quite enjoyed my company at Château Follet."

She quivered. "You left me little choice!"

He raised his brows. "Did I force pleasure upon you? Did I force you to spend like a wanton?"

She attempted to brush by him, but he caught her around the waist. She struggled against him.

"You could have chosen not to enjoy all that you did," he told her. The more she writhed to free herself, the more his groin tightened with arousal. "I would hazard that you still enjoy it."

She pushed against him. "You wish to revel in my disgrace!"

"I wish to exalt it."

She stopped and stared at him.

"You think Château Follet to have been a terrible tragedy to befall our marriage," he said. "I do not."

"Your circumstances there were quite different from mine," she replied, resuming her struggles.

He recalled how she had resisted him in the music room. He had prevailed then. He could prevail now. But he could not be the ogre twice, no matter how much he wished to ravish her. He had spent these months cursing himself, vacillating between guilt and anger, and longing for her presence, craving her body, dreaming of how it would feel to sink himself once more into her wet heat.

"I own I acted abominably," he said instead. "And I intend to be a better husband than I have been."

When he would not release her, her frustration grew. "I think it rather late for such promises!"

Surprised, he let her go. She stumbled out of reach.

"What do you mean?" he demanded. He had expected she would not forgive him immediately, but he had not imagined any other outcome than returning to London with her.

Her brow furrowed in pain, as if her words had cut her as much as they had him. "As I said, we are not suited to each other. I do not think we—I am one who could truly make you happy. We wed out of duty to our families."

"Many men and women marry for such a purpose."

"And I think it wrong. I place no blame upon you. I accepted your proposal knowing full well that you did

171

not love me. But what happened betwixt us at Château Follet has caused irreparable harm to our chances for a happy marriage."

"I disagree—"

"And I think it unnecessary for either one of us to be saddled with such a fate..."

He narrowed his eyes. "What are you suggesting?"

"Given the circumstances, I think a petition for divorce could be easily granted."

Blood pounded in his ears. Divorce? Not once had he contemplated divorce.

"Surely you do not speak of such foolishness in earnest," he said.

She grew defensive. "I do! Adultery is easily grounds for divorce."

"When committed by the wife, yes."

"As you pointed out, I had committed adultery in my heart."

He pressed his lips into a line. Only a woman in utter pain would consider such drastic options. "Have you no sense of what a divorce would mean? The scrutiny, the gossip would fall more harshly upon you than upon me."

"I am prepared to weather it."

She spoke softly, but he believed her as much as if she had made her declaration in the strongest of tones from the hilltops.

"And why would you wish to endure such ignominy?"

"Because I have no wish to be the source of your

marital misery."

"Have I ever said I was miserable?"

"Not in words."

Her response gave him pause. He had lacked the resolve to hold true to his vows, but that was changed. "I have given up my mistress."

"I have no wish for you to cease your affair."

She was being more foolish by the minute, he decided.

"Do you not see that I wish for you to be free to lead the life you desire?" she pressed. "I refuse to be your shackles."

"Do you wish for my freedom or yours?"

She frowned, and he regretted having spoken out of jealousy.

"We would both of us be free," she acknowledged.

"Have you considered what a divorce would do to our families?"

She looked down. "I have."

He had thought divorce an idea that came from the spur of the moment.

"You cannot have fully considered the consequences of seeking a divorce," he said.

"Ours would not be the first, and our families are well connected such that the divorce may be a quiet one, if you will."

"Our families might never forgive us."

"I do not expect that they would forgive us when I have not forgiven myself."

"Damnation, Trudie, if you are not able to forgive

me just yet, I will accept that. But a divorce would be senseless."

"On the contrary, I think it quite sensible. The more I think on it, the more I am convinced it is the best solution, no matter the pain and difficulties that will follow."

He shook his head in disbelief. "I have never known you to be frivolous before. Indeed, it was a quality I quite admired in you till you decided to go to Château Follet. And while your decision to make of me a cuckold infuriated me—"

She groaned and looked away.

He stepped toward her. "But I am prepared to forgive you for that."

"I have no wish for your forgiveness! I do not deserve it!"

"But you wish to punish us both for that?"

"Do you not see the sacrifice I am offering with a divorce?"

"It may be a sacrifice but it is most idiotic!"

Her mouth fell open, and of a sudden, he wanted nothing more than to crush her to him and devour her lips.

"Aye, idiotic, nonsensical, foolhardy."

She straightened in anger.

"What is it you fear, Trudie?" he inquired.

She took a step back from him. "I fear a life of misery for us both."

"I think you fear what you discovered at Château Follet. I think, while you are ashamed of the corporal responses of your body, you desire it, too. You relished all that had transpired at Château Follet."

She faltered but replied, "I may have given into lesser instincts in the moment, but in the clarity of distance, I see no benefit to such indulgences."

"And the benefit of condemning what is natural to your body, to what pleases you?"

She lifted her chin. "So that I might not as easily fall prey to temptations."

"You lie to yourself." He took a step closer and lowered his voice. "I saw you in the throes of ecstasy, my love. Your body desires it no less now than it did then."

"I have the benefit of understanding and better judgment now."

"Do you? I will wager the wanton little harlot lives strong in you still."

He noticed that she trembled a little. Anticipation rose within him.

"If you can prove otherwise, I will grant your divorce."

Chapter Nineteen

LEOPOLD BEHELD HER WIDENED eyes. For a brief moment, he doubted the wisdom of what he had just offered. Perhaps her carnal responses could only be elicited by her debaucher, and that congress with her husband could not be as exciting as congress with a stranger. But even if the answer to his question was not favorable, he had to know if she could be aroused by him.

"I think that quite unnecessary—" she began.

"You fear you will fail my challenge."

He held her gaze, refusing to relinquish her.

"Prevail and I will leave you in peace," he said. After seconds that felt like minutes, he added, "And if you insist on a divorce, consider it your parting gift to me."

After another long silence, she said in a small voice, "Very well."

Slowly, she turned and led him back into the house. At the bottom of the stairs that led to her chamber, she hesitated. She had not looked at him since accepting his challenge. Her gaze still forward, she ascended the stairs.

He followed her, noticing the gentle sway of her hips, the subtle outline of her arse under the fabric of her dress.

Once inside her bedchamber, she still could not look at him. He stood behind her, inches separating them.

"I was a fool, Trudie," he whispered as he slid his fingers from her wrist up arm, "to have taken you for granted."

She sucked in her breath at his words and shivered at his touch.

"P-Perhaps we both have been guilty," she said meekly.

He put his hand upon her shoulder and attempted to knead away the tension there.

"Our wedding night might not have been the best start, but perhaps it could end on a note much improved."

Lowering his head, he kissed the side of her neck and thought he heard a whimper. Sweeping away the soft tendrils at her nape, he trailed kisses all over the back of her neck.

Noticing that she still remained fairly tense, he gently turned her around to face him. "I fully intend to make love to you in the manner you deserve without regard to my own pleasure. You need not fear that I shall force myself upon you."

"Indeed?" she replied in a shaky voice.

"I deserve no pleasure for the part I played at Château Follet. I would pay any penance, Trudie. You have but to name it."

She choked a little. "Truly?"

"Truly."

"What can I do to merit your unequivocal

forgiveness?"

She thought for a moment. "Perhaps you warrant your own spanking."

He stared at her in disbelief at first. A ray of hope bloomed.

"With a wooden paddle to boot," she added.

He chuckled. "I would gladly receive it from your hand, madam. You may take a flogger and whip me within an inch of my life if you wish."

"You know quite well I could do no such thing."

"You could make me pleasure you every night while forbidding me to spend."

Her eyes appeared wet with new tears as she replied with a lifted chin, "P-Perhaps I will."

"Dearest Trudie," he murmured, cupping her face in both his hands. He brushed his lips over hers, felt her breath tremble beneath his mouth. She was divine. He crushed his lips over hers, not realizing how famished he was till he tasted of her. He kissed every part of her mouth, taking mouthfuls, delving deep into the orifice to quench the lust flaming through him.

She was timid at first, but then her reservations gave way like a breached dam. She returned his kiss with equal vigor, equal desperation, equal longing. They consumed one another till the need to breathe necessitated a pause.

"Are you certain you want this?" he murmured atop her lips before kissing his way down her neck.

She arched into him, making the blood rush to his groin. "Yes, Leopold, yes."

As his mouth caressed her throat, her collar, his hands reached behind her for the pins. Frustrated that he could not find them all, he grasped the bodice of her gown and tore it from her. He picked her up, set her against the wall, and locked his mouth to hers once more. His tongue dove into her mouth over and over. He molded his body to hers, seeking the ample curves he had come to find enchanting. His hardness pressed into her belly. It seemed she pressed back.

Resisting the urge to flip up her gown and take her then, he turned her around to face the wall so that he could untie her skirts and petticoats while he kissed the nape of her neck. The muslin pooled upon the ground. He reached around her hip to cup her mound through her shift, the only barrier to that most delightful flesh. He rubbed the shift between her legs and was rewarded with a moan. Soon he could feel dampness upon the garment. He thrust his hips at her, a promise of what was to come. She ground herself into his hand.

"Patience, my love," he whispered into her ear.

She shivered but stayed herself from further movement. Stepping back, he unlaced her stays, then reached for those succulent breasts. He squeezed the orbs through the shift.

"You wish to make me suffer, sir?"

"Of course not."

"Then why will you not ravish me?"

Emotion soared through him, causing his groin to tighten. At that moment, he could not have been more in love with Trudie. He yanked the shift down, baring her body. He was relieved to see she still possessed more fullness than most women. He palmed a buttock, digging his fingers into the succulent flesh. She released a satisfied grunt.

"It would please me greatly to grant your request, my love," he said.

He most likely surprised her with the force and swiftness with which he drew her to the bed.

"My god, you are a sight, Trudie," he groaned, raking his gaze from her neck to her supple thighs. He caressed with hands and mouth every inch of her loveliness before settling his hand between her thighs.

He parted the moist lips below, eliciting a moan, almost a whimper. He smiled as his hand drifted further down and beheld her heaving chest, her nipples hard and ripe. His fingers walked through her folds, finding the slit between and circling it, as his lips pulled a nipple into his mouth. Trudie gasped loudly as his fingers entered her, pressing inside of her. His tongue dragged slowly across her nipple. He slid his fingers out, circling her entry, resisting the urge to press back inside. He teased her as she stared into his eyes, imploring him to enter her again.

"Soon, my love," he growled. "First, I must taste your sweetness."

Lowering his head between her legs, he took in her heady aroma. He parted the lips to her paradise and tongued her there, causing her to shudder. Her thighs brushed against the side of his head. He teased her gently at the base of her entrance, circling it with her tongue before entering, twisting inside of her before withdrawing. She gave a load moan and clutched the bedclothes. He pushed deeper into her, making her gasp. Over and over he worked his tongue upon her, in her, building her pleasure. He dragged his tongue through her wet valley and to that delightful condensation of sensation. He took that swollen nub into his mouth as he sank two fingers into her wet heat.

Her body sprang against him as she uttered something loud and unintelligible. Then, as her back arched, her hips rose against his mouth hard, while he continued to suckle her bud of pleasure, and then she dropped to the bed as his fingers curled, sliding out from inside of her for a brief moment before driving back into her once more.

"Oh, Leopold!" she cried.

He exalted at the cry of his name. His fingers slipped in and out of her wetness easily. She shifted below him, left and right, up and down. He did his best to contain her while at the same time freeing the carnal within her. His mouth tiring, but his commitment unwavering, he was driven to break her, to feel her submit to him wholly and completely. He listened for the hunger to take her, for her climax to claim her as his fingers and tongue wrought rapture through her.

Minutes later, her body bucked and shivered as her moans turned into cries. The moment was before him and he did not demur, intent on delivering an ecstasy that would leave no doubts that she desired him, needed him. She arched off the bed, thrusting into his mouth while his fingers drove deep inside her.

"My God, My God!" she cried.

He rode her out, licking, sucking, his fingers gliding in and out of her, feeling her nectar flow around him. When it seemed she could endure no more, he eased his ministrations and withdrew his fingers. He drank in the sight of her as she melted into the bed, a blush gracing her cheeks, her eyes bright and dilated. His own arousal pressed painfully against his trousers, but he let her have a moment of calm as he removed his coat, waistcoat, and cravat.

"I suppose you have proved your point," she murmured with lowered lashes. "I am a wanton little harlot."

"And I would have you in no other way, my love," he growled as he climbed over her. He kissed her, pressing into her mouth all the desire pent up within him. She returned his kiss, which fueled his ardor even higher.

He rolled her atop him and pulled her legs up so that she straddled him. Cupping the back of her head, he shoved his tongue between her lips. His hips thrust at her, his hardness seeking her wet heat.

To his surprise, she reached for the buttons of his fall. He would not release her mouth, but she managed to undo a few. When he could no longer deny the craving between his legs, he allowed her to undo his fall completely and helped her to free his shaft. Before he could object, she had lowered her head and engulfed his erection.

Bloody hell…

It was the most marvelous sensation, the exquisite rapture humbling him. Dear, dear Trudie.

"You must use me for your pleasure," he managed to whisper, though every nerve begged for her to cradle his erection in her mouth and never let go. He pulled her off him.

"Come," he said, "ride me as one rides a steed, as you had done at Château Follet."

He lifted her hips, held in place with one hand while he straightened himself, then guided her gently down. Her eyes widened as the head of his rod pierced her folds. Gripping both her hips with both hands, he settled her further down him. Her lips parted as her tight tunnel swallowed him. When she had taken his length, he ground her against his pelvis. Her eyes rolled toward the back of her head.

He drew in a long breath to steady himself. If he allowed himself, his pleasure would burst through within minutes. Gradually, he lifted her hips so that she slid up his length before he pressed her back down. After several minutes, she found his rhythm and moved with him. Her breath quickened, her brow furrowed. "My God, you are marvelous," he breathed.

Her gasps grew louder and more frequent. He thrust his hips more vigorously at her, seeking to bury himself as deep within her as he could, his sight filled with her bosom, the large orbs bouncing up and down. The sound of wet flesh slapping upon flesh filled the room with her gasps and cries.

"Leopold…" she cried before her body erupted into shudders.

He rammed himself into her, bucking against her as she flexed and quaked about him. The tension coiled within him shot through his shaft as he felt her body ready to collapse. Holding her aloft, he thrust into her until his desire had completely drained into her before allowing her to crumple atop him. They lay, breast to breast, breathing hard, their perspiration mingled together.

"Your pardon," he said when they had both collected their breaths. "I ought not have spent, but I can pleasure you still…May I?"

Turning her head, she looked at him. "Are you asking permission of me? Is that customary for masters at Château Follet to question their students?"

"Very little is customary at Château Follet." He paused to search her countenance. "Do you—would you—wish to continue the lessons we had started at Château Follet?"

Her lashes lowered, and the ensuing silence was agony to him. She looked up at him. "Yes."

His heart raced anew. "Then you no longer wish for a divorce?"

"It was agreed that you would grant it to me only if I prevailed against what you deemed my true nature."

"It is one matter to succumb to the carnal that resides in all humans, another to willfully desire it, and to desire it with me."

"I desire it, Leopold."

No statement had ever sounded sweeter to him. "Then you mean to forgive me?"

She spoke with a tremor. "I suppose I do."

He caught her hand in his tightly, hoping that his shaft would recover soon that he might claim her once more, and ease the bursting of his heart through the heat of congress. He kissed her hand.

"I vow, as your husband, to indulge your every desire, to bring you relentless pleasure, and to cherish and love you, my love, for better, for worse, for richer, for poorer, in sickness and in health, till death do us part."

Her eyes glimmered. She pressed his hand in return. "This, too, shall be my vow, dear Leopold."

With his free hand, he cupped her chin and raised her lips to meet his. As he kissed her, drinking in the happiness that Trudie was his wife and he her husband, he silently acknowledged Château Follet, grateful and excited that they might find many occasions to return.

OTHER TITLES BY
GEORGETTE BROWN

Steamy Regency Collection
An Indecent Wager (Book #1)
Surrendering to the Rake (Book #2)
That Wicked Harlot (Book #3)
Tempting a Marquess (Book #4)
Tempting a Marquess for Christmas (Book #5)

Other
Pride, Prejudice & Pleasure
The Countess and the Rake